Merger
of
Evil

Shannon Ryan

Merger of Evil

Shannon Ryan

Broken Typewriter Press • Cedar Rapids

Cover Design by Blair Gaunt
https://bygauntt.com/

Edited by Adam J Whitlatch
https://www.adamjwhitlatch.com/

Broken Typewriter Press
https://broken.typewriter.press/

ISBN 978-1-940509-31-0

Version 0.4.9

For Stacie, who challenged me to write a female protagonist so she could have a character to identify with in my books. I proceeded to write a character completely different from her.

Acknowledgment

This book could not have been made without help from Dylan Moonfire, who spends time making my books look good when he could be working on his own stories; The Noble Pen writing group who read my awful first drafts; and Catherine Schaff-Stump, who encourages me to keep going.

1

Miss America

Ottoel sat in the Cloud Nine conference room waiting for his superior. The room was a sedate beige like a nineties Ramada, and on one wall, large, friendly windows displayed a view of Infinity.

He was annoyed at being called back, having asked for the first half of the twenty-first century off. He'd put in a hard shift during the 1900s, and he wanted to try one of those "staycations" which were getting popular down on Earth.

A pot of coffee and some cups sat in the middle of the table. Ottoel poured himself a cup and sniffed it. Cold and stale. As a lowly guardian angel, Ottoel probably should take the initiative to make a fresh pot, but instead he just chucked the cup in the trash. He whispered his favorite line from Jason Sizemore's *Cashiers*. "I'm supposed to have the day off."

Archangel Lucael entered, looking pissed off as usual. "I suppose you know why you're here."

As Ottoel was the only other person in the conference room, he assumed he was the one being addressed. "Actually, I have no idea. I was on vacation."

An annoyed look on Lucael's face told Ottoel that his superior was unconcerned with the loss of his vacation. "Back in the nineties you..." He paused and made a face like he had eaten something vile. "You made a deal with the father of a dying baby, Canadian Cobra —"

"America Mustang."

"Whatever. We were going to have her deal with the Calltelestar Peopleconnect situation. But some complications have arisen."

"So, somebody screwed up?" Ottoel said. Even as the words left his mouth, he realized he'd made a horrible mistake, especially if someone important had made that error, someone like Lucael.

While he didn't exactly glare at Ottoel, the temperature in the room seemed to lower a notch. Ottoel wasn't sure if he was just empathetically sensing Lucael's irritation or if the angel had literally sent a chill through the room. Lucael was in a higher angelic choir and probably had the ability to control local weather. "Yes," he said finally. "I suppose you could say that is correct."

Ottoel suddenly got the feeling that if Lucael had the choice, he would happily make Ottoel his scapegoat rather than accept any of the blame himself.

"I'd like you to go down there," Lucael said. "Speak with her directly."

"You want me to go down to Earth?" Ottoel asked. "You want me to go down to Earth and talk to a human?" Guardian angels pulled shifts on Earth all the time, but they usually stayed invisible, offering small coincidences or signs to get a human's attention. They didn't go around directly offering advice. That was not done.

"I need someone down there to manage the Callte-lestar situation, and you're the only angel I can trust."

This actually amazed Ottoel. If he'd been asked a century ago what Lucael's opinion of him was, he'd have guessed the answer would be, "barely adequate." But then again, maybe Ottoel was just suffering from low self-esteem.

○ ○ ○

Amy was getting fired today. She had come in a tad bit late, as she tended to do, and found her supervisor waiting to tell her, "David Graves wants to have a word in the small conference room as soon as possible." She had worked at Calltelestar for three weeks as a Teleservice Representative, and David only talked to anyone so insignificant for one purpose, especially on Friday.

The first thing you learned about David was he would be the one to fire you. Technically he was her supervisor's boss and a division head, but he fired everyone in the building, no matter what division they worked for. They said he took quite a bit of pleasure in firing people. Amy sometimes wondered who would fire David Graves if they wanted him gone.

Then again, that might be why he'd risen all the way to partner; no one had the authority to fire him. Rumor said that his predecessor, Matt Rose, had tried to fire him. Graves had assaulted Rose at work, and soon after, Rose had died under mysterious circumstances. The company gossips claimed he'd beaten Rose to death with a hammer in the basement of the building, which was ridiculous, of course.

She actually found him charismatic, in a used car salesman sort of way, and she knew plenty of her coworkers thought he was cute, even if he was unavailable. He apparently had a scary jealous girlfriend—

like a burn down your garage and tell you, "Your family is next," scary girlfriend.

Amy's workspace was one of six, crammed onto an eight-foot table. Calltelestar didn't believe in full size cubicles or desks for customer service employees. They just got a divider, which gave them a tiny bit of privacy but buffered sound enough that the people they called wouldn't hear a noisy call center in the background. Once again, the night shift person had left candy wrappers all over the table. Amy had complained about it a few times, they weren't even supposed to eat at their workstations, but no one seemed to care.

She logged on to her computer to show she was in the building—might as well get paid for one more hour—and left the shelter of her gray privacy shield. Her heels clicked on the polished terrazzo tiles as she walked across the call floor. Calltelestar might pay their employees like shit, but when it came to amenities like flooring, no expense was spared.

The small conference room next to Graves' office was exclusively reserved for firing people individually or in small groups. The room's decor seemed to be based on the same lifeless gray as their privacy dividers on the call floor. At least there were a few plants in the conference room, but despite being plastic, they looked almost ready to die. Where did you even buy plants like that? After making herself comfortable, she waited.

She had to admit, she winced a little when he came through the door, slamming it open with casual force. She pretended his loud entrance hadn't made her jump.

He wore an expensive suit that barely hid his muscular build. His baby face and clear blue eyes make him look closer to his mid-twenties, like her, though she guessed him to be probably a decade older. He leaned down to offer her a handshake, and she got a good look at the perfectly manicured nails on his large hands.

4

"Good morning, Miss America," Graves said.

Amy cringed at the use of her given name, especially with "Miss" in front of it. It made her sound like a beauty contestant and made her want to commit murder. He must have done it just to screw with her. No one in Iowa said things like, "Miss First-Name." She considered that mainly a southern thing, and he didn't sound like he came from the South.

Her father had given her the name America. He reasoned that since his surname was Love, he should name his daughter after two things he loved, his country and his car. Hence, she was baptized America Mustang Love. If she'd been a boy, her name would have been Ronald Shelby after Ronald Reagan and, yes, the car. She loved her father with all her heart, which was the only thing stopping her having it legally changed.

"Please, just call me Amy."

"All right, Amy. Do you have any idea why you're here today?"

She shrugged. "I think I have a general sort of idea. You're going to—"

"Because of your stepmother."

Amy felt her mouth drop open. "What? How do you even know my stepmother?"

"I don't really. She called me the other day. She actually offered me a bribe to tell her if your employment status changed. She was quite insistent about it."

Amy hated the idea of her stepmother bribing her employer for dirt. The idea of that bitch sticking her nose into Amy's business made her nauseous. "She's a demon straight out of Hell."

Graves leaned forward and raised an eyebrow. His chair creaked attentively. "Really?"

Amy took a deep breath to get her temper under control. She forced herself to sound calm. "Well, not really. It's just a metaphor."

He sat back in his chair. "Oh, well, the world is full of not-so-nice people." He looked a bit disappointed.

5

"I hope you told her to mind her own business."

"Actually, I took the bribe." He flashed her a boyish grin that actually made her warm to him for a moment before remembering what a loathsome, despicable human being he was. "She seemed like a pleasant enough lady, and while I really didn't need her money, I thought it would be impolite not to take it. Maybe I'll buy myself a nice bottle of Scotch. This is Calltelestar. We do have a reputation to maintain."

She felt her temper rise again. "A reputation? A reputation as what? A bunch of assholes?"

She thought she'd crossed a line with that comment, but Graves didn't seem to mind. Instead, he flashed her that damn grin again. "Our reputation precedes us."

"So, you're going to spy on me for my stepmother. She might seem nice to you, but she's quite an atrocious person. I'm sure you'll regret doing business with her."

He shook his head. "No. I'm not going to spy on you. That would be way too much work. I'm going to fire you. That way, I can take my bribe and immediately tell your stepmother that your employment condition has changed. If you attempt to seek unemployment, we will, of course, contest your benefits. If you attempt to appeal, we can furnish adequate levels of proof that you have been urinating at your work area."

"What? That's totally gross. If you're going to make up things about me, could you at least make up something believable? Women don't just go around peeing on floors."

He shrugged. "We must know different types of women."

"But why are you firing me because of my stepmother? I can't control what my stepmother does. It's not fair." She found his attitude rather annoying. If she actually wanted to work at Calltelestar, she might have even been mad about it.

Graves smiled and took out a thick bundle of paper. "In that case, I'll have to point you to page forty-five of our employee manual." He actually had an employee manual ready for this occasion. He opened it to a bookmarked page and tapped his finger next to the large text within. "Calltelestar Peopleconnect Employee Handbook, Section 10. We don't care if you think it is fair."

Amy didn't bother to read further. The section heading held enough information to get the point across, despite going on at length. "Okay, I've seen enough. Do you really have to tell them I pee on the floor?"

Graves shook his head. "We will return a form with vague language about you being difficult to work with. We'll only push the urination thing if you go after your rightful unemployment payments. And believe me when I say you're getting off easy. You'd be amazed at the amount of people we fire for having sexual relations with inanimate objects." He chuckled to himself. "You know, Miss America—"

"Amy."

"I really am doing you a favor. I'm sure you don't really want to work here, and this place has a way of changing you. You might not believe it, but I used to be a really nice guy."

She shook her head at this logic. "Thanks a lot, asshole." She really wanted to yell and swear and cause a scene, but she didn't, because he was right. She really didn't want to work here, or anywhere. At some point, after about her thirtieth menial job, the little flame of Midwesterner work ethic inside her had been extinguished forever. By Iowa standards, that probably made her the laziest person in the state.

Graves stood, signaling their meeting had come to an end. "Trust me. This is for your own good. You seem like a smart young lady. There must be better places you can work. You don't want to get stuck here."

A stack of cardboard boxes sat by the door. Graves picked one up and passed it to her. "Here you go. Security will meet you by your desk. You can collect your things, and they'll escort you out."

She nodded. "I know the drill. I've been fired from nicer places than this." This wasn't even an insult so much as a simple statement of fact.

Amy did the Calltelestar walk of shame back to her desk with her cardboard box. Co-workers who had gossiped with her in the parking lot or gone for after work drinks with her now hid their eyes. She didn't care so much about them. She was too busy thinking about horrible things she would do to her stepmother.

Then again, she knew she wouldn't really do anything to her stepmother. She didn't like the woman—that was an understatement—but dismemberment seemed a bit harsh, and would, undoubtedly, upset her father, who was guilty of nothing more than marrying the Devil.

Besides, she had better things to do with her time than petty revenge. It was 10:30 AM. There had to be a bar open somewhere. She wondered how many drinks she could put on her father's credit card before her stepmother canceled it.

○ ○ ○

Fired and exit interview done, Amy was in the bar before 11 AM. She enjoyed a good day drunk, but she knew to pace herself. Too much one way, and she might experience sobriety. Too much the other might meant waking up on the floor, or in some creepy rando's bed. Having experienced that once, she wasn't going to let it happen again.

She didn't really care about Calltelestar, but she had this deal with her father. As long as she was employed, he'd take care of her credit card and rent, as her jobs tended toward the minimum wage, and he was a rich attorney. Well, "rich" was a relative term.

8

He represented a lot of millionaire farmers, and he could probably buy a state senator or two if he wanted, but he wasn't buying a jet anytime soon.

At her core, Amy worried she was a failure. She was a parasite living off her father, probably no better than her stepmother. Her father thought working a job, any job, would make her feel better about herself. He was wrong. The jobs she got were a constant reminder that she would never amount to anything.

Of course, now she didn't have a job, which meant she was in danger of losing her Des Moines apartment. Without a place to live, she'd have to go home to Holstein, Iowa, population 1500. Her father would give her a few weeks to find employment, like he always did, but that meant looking for a job, which was the worst. Supposedly, employment rates were currently high, and it was easy to get a job. However, she'd burned her bridges with a number of Des Moines businesses, most of the larger employers in fact. She'd even been banned from McDonald's, not just as an employee but as a customer too.

She missed the fries.

Amy didn't usually hang out in dive bars, stewing about her circumstances, but The Bolt Hole was the perfect place for it, one of those quiet, neighborhood bars catering to factory workers hiding from their spouses after a long shift. She liked to go there when she needed some alone time. Unlike other bars in the area, The Bolt Hole wasn't going to try to ruin her day with a local band, karaoke night, or—she shuddered—line dancing.

The bartender, a fatherly guy named Roy, came over and nodded at her rum and Diet Coke. "How are you doing, Amy?"

"I'm doing great, Roy. I just got fired, which means if I can't find a new job, my dad will probably make me move home, and I'll end up married to a farmer who works twelve hours a day. Once a week, we'll go to the Corner Tap for fun, at least until I poop out kids to help him in the fields. And they'll all have those stupid biblical names... Jebediah, Ezekiel, Barnabas, Jesus—"

"Um... I meant do you need—"

"And you know what? I'd probably be fine with that. But that wouldn't be good enough for Patty."

"Okay."

"Patty's my evil stepmother. She never gets tired of reminding me about how successful and pretty and independent her daughter, Debbie, is. So, I decided my best course of action was to get the hell out of Holstein, so I didn't have to listen to Patty anymore. I did the good daughter thing. I went to college—"

"Hey, I'm sorry, but someone at the other side of the bar needs a drink." He hurried away to a group of third-shift workers enjoying some after-work beers. They wore matching blue coveralls, not very fashion forward, but she idly wondered if the place where they worked was hiring. She looked good in blue.

She wished Roy had stayed long enough for her to order a glass of water. A tall glass of cold water about once an hour was a key ingredient to remaining tipsy but not sloppy drunk. She should probably just go home and drink, but she was leaning toward morose anyway, no need to put herself in isolation. Plus, didn't only alcoholics drink alone at home? At least she didn't have that to worry about.

By noon, the third shift workers had gone home, and the business lunch crowd had moved in. She listened to a group at a nearby table, coworkers arguing about whether country legend Bubba Strayhorn was still alive. One guy was sure he was dead, but someone else claimed to have tickets to an upcoming show in Minneapolis. Amy didn't really care, but her dad loved Bubba Strayhorn. She was sure she'd know if he were dead.

Amy spent several hours' worth of rum and Diet Cokes playing on her phone, trying to maintain relationships with people she didn't talk to anymore by liking baby pictures—you *had* to like baby pictures even the ugly ones.

The day drained into evening and the sun went down. The lull of the afternoon ended as the nightly drinkers moved in and took over. A guy walked up to her and said, "I'm Nelson. What are you drinking?" To her, he looked like a typical college meathead looking to score. She was *so* not interested.

"Fuck off, Nelson," Amy replied. Nelson moved down the bar to the next woman sitting by herself, a little red-haired girl that didn't look old enough to be in a bar.

A few minutes later, another guy sat down on the bar stool next to her. She was about to tell him to also fuck off when he waved to Roy the bartender, and without asking, Roy brought him a beer.

"This one's on the house, officer."

"Thanks, Roy."

Amy turned toward the new guy. The man seemed the opposite of Nelson, six inches shorter and maybe one hundred pounds lighter. He had a Latino complexion and dressed neatly. He had a bit of a cowboy thing going—boots, denim shirt and pants, and a black leather vest. After many drinks, her filter must have been down, and she spat out, "You're a cop?"

He nodded. "Yeah. I helped Roy with a disturbance a couple nights ago. I'm off duty, but I thought I'd stop by and make sure he hadn't had any more trouble." He looked around. "And while I was here, I was hoping to scope out some cute guys."

"Wait, you're a gay, Latino cop? I didn't think that was allowed in Iowa." Amy's father hung around with lots of rural sheriffs and judges, and in her experience, people working in law enforcement hadn't been very open-minded on issues of race and sexuality.

He shrugged. "There are problems in the system. That's part of the reason I decided to become a police officer. People need to see more people like me in a uni-

11

form, especially the other guys in uniform." He smiled at her. "You have a good evening, ma'am."

The cop took his beer to a table, and Amy settled up with the bartender, leaving him a generous tip for putting up with her all day.

As she turned to get down from her stool, she saw Nelson leaning over the young girl. So creepy. She knew she should mind her own business, but she strained to hear what they were saying. Something about buying her drinks and her not appreciating him. He pounded on the bar a couple times.

The girl got up from the bar and headed for the door at a pretty good pace for the heels she was wearing, but Nelson followed her, either not getting the hint or not caring to.

Amy got up from the barstool, but she stumbled a bit. Okay, maybe she was a little more drunk than she'd intended to be, but there was fuckery afoot. She made her way to the door and got outside, just as the redhead was saying, "Please, leave me alone."

Amy put her hand on Nelson's shoulder and spun him around. "You heard the lady," she said. "Leave her alone." She knew she should feel scared, should be afraid of this huge guy, but she was really pissed off. "This girl's like sixteen years old."

"I'm twenty-three. I'm a med student," the girl responded. Amy squinted. No, she still didn't look it.

Nelson loomed over her. "You females are all alike, aren't you? You think you're better than us."

Taking into account Nelson's size, Amy slipped her hand into her purse and made sure she knew where her pepper spray was. Ignoring Nelson, she turned to the girl and said, "I think it's time for you to go." She also wanted to give the girl a lecture about drinking alone, but since Amy had been doing the same thing, she held her tongue. When the girl didn't move, she glared at her and said, "Run!"

The girl turned and ran.

Nelson glared at her. "You stupid bitch. You know how many drinks I bought her?"

"Two or three?" Amy guessed. He hadn't been around her that long.

"Well, they're expensive."

"Uh huh." Amy slipped past him and walked fast for her car. She was probably too tipsy to drive, but she could lock herself in. But when she got there, she stopped. He'd followed her, and if she wanted to get her keys, she'd have to let go of her pepper spray. She turned to face him, to make it easier to spray him if necessary.

He slapped the top of her car. "Look, you bitch. I just wasted my whole night, and you totally cock blocked me. I think you at least owe me a blow job."

Amy found this negotiation tactic so ludicrous, she forgot for a minute how scary he looked. All she could think was to ask, "How, in your mind, does that make any sense?" She might have laughed at him, just a little.

He slapped her car again. "Listen, bitch—"

"I think you need to calm down," said a voice behind them. Over Nelson's bulk, Amy hadn't even seen anyone approach. It was the cop from the bar. She recalculated her previous estimation. He was at least eight inches shorter than Nelson, but for a little guy, he had a voice of authority.

"Why don't you mind your own business?" Nelson said. Then he put his hand out to push the smaller man away.

The smaller man sidestepped Nelson's push, grabbed his arm, twisted it, and rode him down to the pavement, shoving his knee in the bigger man's back. In the blink of an eye, he'd zip-tied Nelson's hands behind his back. He stood and brushed himself off. "Are you okay, ma'am?"

Amy nodded. "I'm good." She looked down at Nelson. "That was... impressive."

"Muscle memory. Training. It's my job."

Amy had thought he was on the small side for a cop, but apparently muscle memory and training could make up for that.

He pulled a wallet from his back pocket and handed her a business card. It had a picture of him in full uniform on it. "Holden Ramirez. You looked like you needed a little help."

"Thanks, Officer Ramirez." She took his card and put it in her pocket.

"Call me Holden."

"Okay, Holden. I'm Amy."

"Hey, what about me?" Nelson said from the ground, rolling over on his side. "This is very uncomfortable."

"If you're really good," Holden said, "I won't put you in a jail cell overnight. Promise you'll be a good boy and go home, right now, and you can sleep in your own bed."

Nelson looked really upset, like he wanted to make trouble, but he said through clenched teeth, "Yeah, okay."

Holden took out a little key and undid the zip tie around Nelson's wrists. "Now, go home before I change my mind."

Nelson looked pissed, but he must have decided that Holden's threat had some teeth behind it. He hurried to the other side of the parking lot and got into a red SUV. As he drove away, he flipped them the bird and shouted something about pigs and sluts.

Holden slipped the oversized zip tie into his vest pocket. "Charming fellow. Known him long?"

"He was getting really aggressive with that little girl at the end of the bar. I... decided to get involved."

"And you forgot there was a police officer across the room who could have helped you?"

Amy shrugged. "Apparently." She felt like she needed to make an excuse. "They were leaving, I didn't want to waste time."

"Come with me. I'll give you a ride home."

"Oh, no." She shook her head. "I'll just get an Uber. I don't want to ruin your evening or anything."

"Don't worry about it. I only went out tonight because I hardly know anyone outside people from work. I just moved here."

"I... I just... Um. Now that this is over, I'm feeling a little lightheaded." She turned and puked into the gutter. It was nothing but net—she didn't get any on her clothes, she didn't even have to wipe her mouth.

As she waited to see if anything else was on its way up, Holden came over and patted her back. At first, she winced at the contact, but it felt reassuring. "Feeling better?" he asked. "Now, let's get you home."

Amy liked to think of herself as an independent woman who didn't need anyone's help, but Nelson had shaken her enough that she was willing to swallow her pride. Logically, she had to admit she was probably safer with the cop who had just helped her than an anonymous Uber driver, but there was one thing bothering her. "Just one more question. Why are you carrying around giant zip ties?"

"They're actually plastic handcuffs, not as bulky as the metal ones. You can even unlock them with a handcuff key. If you have a deep inside pocket, they don't even ruin the line of your outfit, so I keep some on hand for situations like this—off duty, but a civilian needs assistance."

Out of Midwestern politeness, Amy felt required to say, "I guess I could use a ride home, if I'm not putting you out. I don't want to ruin your evening."

○ ○ ○

By the time they pulled up to Amy's apartment, they'd shared the abridged versions of their life stories. Holden was twenty-five, almost as old as her. He'd been born and raised in Phoenix, like his father before him. His mother immigrated from Mexico as a child; she hadn't taught him Spanish, but he could

15

make killer tamales. After getting his criminal justice degree, he'd worked as a reserve police officer in Arizona, but he had to move to get a full-time job. He'd just broken up with his cowboy ex—apparently Holden was into rugged men who wore lots of denim—so he decided to make the move.

Amy told Holden about living in Debbie's shadow, dealing with her awful stepmother, bailing on college, and subsisting on low-paying jobs like food service and telemarketing.

Holden parked his car outside her building's front door.

"Thanks, Holden. I really appreciate you coming all this way."

"Actually, I only live half a block from here, so it wasn't even an inconvenience. Are you okay? Do you need me to walk you up?"

"I think I'll be okay." Amy opened the door and fell out onto the sidewalk.

A moment later, Holden lifted her off the rough concrete. After picking a cigarette butt off her face, he carried her up the two flights of stairs to her apartment. He held her up, balancing her against the wall, while she found her keys and unlocked the door. Walking her inside, he carefully led her through piles of dirty clothes and dropped her on her bed. "I think that counts as leg day," he said, collapsing beside her.

"Are you sure you're not trying to seduce me?" Amy asked.

"Quite sure. You're not my type, not enough stubble. But if you're very nice, I may help you get your shoes off."

"I like you, Holden. We should totally hang out." She fell asleep.

○ ○ ○

Across town, David Graves took the elevator to the basement of the Calltelestar building, something

16

impossible to do without a secret elevator code, something that could get you killed if you weren't supposed
to be there. He carried a briefcase, which he never
used except on nights like these.

When he arrived in the anteroom of the basement
church, only the president of the company, Randy
Clarke, waited there. "You're running a bit late, aren't
you?"

The anteroom floor was black marble, as were
the walls. It held benches (black) so the older members
of their cabal could sit down while they dressed, and
lockers (black) for stowing personal items. David un-
snapped the latches on the leather briefcase, took out
his long, black cloak and put it on. He grabbed a
wicked-looking dagger—a ten-inch curved assassin's
blade with little devils and tortured souls engraved all
over the hilt—from the case and tucked it into his
robes. "I'm ready. Let's go."

They walked into the inner church, where the other members of the coven waited, mainly the other vice
presidents and board members of the company, though
you couldn't really tell them apart, as they were all
wearing cloaks and hoods as well. While traditional,
David sometimes wondered if this was a best practice,
as it would be hard to spot an impostor.

Just like the antechamber, the motif of the room
was black. Black marble floors ran to black marble
walls. Black marble walls and black marble pillars
held up a black ceiling. Unfortunately, the black ceiling
was merely painted fiberboard tiles, because suspended ceilings were just too practical in large commercial
buildings.

Dark gray marble inlaid into the black made a pattern in the floor, a huge pentagram inscribed in a circle. In the center of that circle, like a pillar, stood a
computer server in a large metal rack. Various LEDs
blinked, indicating the server was doing things.

In addition to the computer, David was also keenly
aware of a large safe set into the back wall of the

room. In that safe, along with several million dollars in cash, was a document which Julie, the HR demon, had tricked David into signing—the document which said Calltelestar owned his soul.

Randy took his place next to Charlie Stevens, the chairman of the board and the father of David's girlfriend, Raven. The two had started the company together with David's predecessor, Matt Rose.

They started to chant in Latin. David had memorized the chants, and though he was learning Latin, he really couldn't follow all that closely. He knew they roughly translated to the lyrics of the song, *Hey Mickey*, by Toni Basil, except substituting "Satan" for "Mickey." In fact, when he'd first seen the Latin to English translation, David wondered if they hadn't just stolen the song and translated it to Latin to avoid any copyright claims. Just because they only said the verse in secret in a locked basement didn't mean the music industry wouldn't find out. And despite being vengeful Satanists with attorneys on their board of directors who specialized in litigation, they knew enough not to mess with the music industry.

While David understood the power and purpose of ritual, the whole process was just opening up a conduit to Hell, which they could have done with the computer and saved everyone a late night in the office. However, Charlie Stevens believed they needed to get together to download the sacrifices. Later, when all the ceremony was over, they'd no doubt go eat at Perkins.

They got to David's part of the ceremony, which he'd inherited when he'd killed Matt Rose. He said two phrases of Latin, pulled the nasty-looking dagger from his robes, walked over to the server, and drew a shallow cut across his forearm. He smeared a bit of blood on the blade and then plugged a USB cable into the tiny port on the hilt of the dagger.

After typing his password into the console, he ran a couple of commands, again ones he had memorized.

This would channel the micro-souls stored in the computer into the dagger, and on to Hell.

Apparently, the idea had come from Internet micro-transactions. Instead of sacrificing whole people to the Devil, which was messy and generated all kinds of scrutiny from the authorities, Calltelestar stole tiny portions of people's lives—the working days of its menial employees and the time of the people they called —for the glory of Satan. Occasionally, a bug in the system would kill someone they called, but any employee who heard someone die over the phone would immediately be fired so they wouldn't see a pattern.

While he was beginning to get the hang of dark wizardry, David didn't understand how the technology worked. How did you store one thousandth of a person's soul on a hard drive? How did you suck it through a telephone? They had this tech guy who apparently had figured it all out. That guy looked like a proper Satanist—he had pointed red sideburns and everything.

The server seemed to be working slowly today. David was about to try the final command again, when an error message popped up. "File Not Found." He turned back to his black-robed colleagues. "It says file not found."

He was greeted with silence.

After a moment, Amanda Caraway, inventor of the extended automotive warranties call, said, "Maybe you should try turning it off and on again?"

David nodded. Fortunately, their servers ran Windows—a Satanist inside Microsoft had actually been responsible for Windows Server 2016 as well as Windows Vista—so David knew how to shut it down. Then he got another message. "Now it says boot media not found."

Charlie Stevens said, "Where's that guy from IT, the one with the sideburns?"

Randy hung his head. "I had him killed."

"What? Why?" Stevens asked.

19

"To protect our trade secrets. Like Ivan the Terrible blinding the architect of that cathedral. We have all the source code."

"Oh, well then," Stevens said in his sarcastic voice. "That's wonderful. Does anyone here know what to do with source code that can steal people's souls through the telephone?" He paused for a moment, and when no one spoke up, he said, "I'm sure we could just call a temp agency and get any old programmer to get our one-of-a-kind computer system up and running. You know, Dick Storm was ready to trade his whole company just so he could get a taste of our soul throughput. We'd just started negotiations to merge with Mediastorm."

Randy opened his mouth, but he was literally struck dumb.

David felt bad for him. Mediastorm held a monopoly providing cable and Internet services for most of the state of Iowa and stood as a testament to how far bribery of state and local officials could take a company. A merger with Mediastorm could be a billion-dollar deal.

Stevens growled to Clarke, "You know, Randy, that was such a genius move, I'm thinking of having you killed to protect the company."

2

Day Labor for Rogue Websites

Sunlight broke through the curtains of Amy's studio apartment, revealing a sea of fabric. Racks overloaded with dresses and skirts, tops and pants, trailed down to meet the rising tide of dirty clothes below. A bed dominated the center of the room, an island of heaped blankets and sheets that—theoretically—contained Amy.

At 8:30 AM, Amy's phone blared, "The Bitch Is Back," the ringtone she reserved for her stepmother. Amy's hand shot out from beneath the blankets, groped until it found her phone, and sent the call to voice mail.

Ten minutes later, the phone rang again, and once again she sent it to voice mail.

When the song rang out again another ten minutes later, she pulled the phone under the covers. "What?"

"America, your father told me you were fired yesterday." That was Patty, all right, blunt and to the point. No chance of niceties or small talk. Of course, Amy knew she was lying. Her father hadn't found out about her termination from Calltelestar. That had been Patty's doing, bribing Mr. Graves.

"Yeah, so what? And don't call me America. Call me Amy." Hungover and grumpy at being woken, Amy wasn't in the mood for Patty's shit. "And why do you always call so early? Don't you sleep?"

"I just got off the phone with Debbie. She's been in the office for a half hour already. And she went for a run. When was the last time you exercised? Your figure, such as it is, won't last forever, you know?"

"Wait... What's wrong with my—"

"You know the deal. Your father will pay your rent and credit card as long as you have a job."

The nuclear deterrent. If Amy lost her job, she would have to move back in with her father and stepmother, in Holstein. No clubs. No shops. No fun.

Amy shuddered with anger. "You can't blame me for that. Calltelestar fires, like, ten people a day just for fun. Besides, I was just fired yesterday. Just give me a few weeks to find a new job. Besides, it was *your* fault—"

"Now you're blaming me for losing a job. That's just sad, Amy. I've discussed it with your father, and we've decided that you have until the end of this week to find a new job. Then you'll have to move home."

Amy couldn't believe what she was hearing. They'd always given her a month or more to look for work. "But it's already Tuesday! No one is going to hire me in three days."

"You'll have to figure out something. Get off your butt and do the legwork."

"It doesn't work that way. You fill out applications online—"

Patty continued, undeterred. "You don't need to get a perfect job with your father paying your bills. At your age, I..." Amy pulled the phone from her ear so Patty could have some time to espouse on her hard times as a showgirl in Branson. She didn't need a reminder that after the death of her mother, her otherwise quite intelligent father had thrown himself at the first big-boobed floozy—an old-fashioned word, but one that fit Patty beautifully.

If Patty was serious, she'd have to start looking immediately. Of course, there were always jobs available, but Amy preferred one which wouldn't make her work too hard, smell like fries, or even worse, cut into her evenings. Hopefully her blue jacket was clean; she didn't have time for dry cleaning.

Realizing Patty's monologue was winding down, Amy stopped the mental assembly of her job-search outfit and returned the phone to her ear. "...the headpiece alone was twenty pounds, but I didn't complain. You need to take responsibility for your life. There's no reason you can't act like an adult. You can't live on your father's money forever, you know. You understand that, don't you?"

Amy understood the subtext. As soon as her father died, Patty was going to take all his money and move somewhere nice, and Patty's plans did not include continuing to pay Amy's credit card bill every month. As Amy had never worked at a job that would pay both her rent and expenses, hopefully Dad had many good decades in front of him. "Yes. I totally do. In fact, I'm going to go out and look right now," she said quickly and hung up.

Yawning, Amy opened the web browser on her phone to look for job listings. She proceeded to fall asleep for another two hours. By noon, she was up and dressed, a breakfast Diet Coke in her hand and ready to start thinking about her dilemma.

But first, she picked her dirty bras from the floor. She could put off job searching for a few more minutes if she started a load of blacks. One of the few advantages of her apartment was the tiny washer and dryer, allowing her to wash her clothes at leisure rather than standing guard over a coin-operated machine in a dirty basement to make sure no one dumped her wet clothes on the floor and stole her dryer.

One of the wires had started to poke out from her favorite black bra, so in a last resort to save it, she tried super-gluing the wire in. Once the glue seemed dry, she put all her bras in a delicates bag and threw it in the washer.

She looked at her phone again and searched "get job fast." The first result was a ten-step plan for getting a job. Amy figured she had no time for anything that took more than three steps, possibly four, but definitely not ten. The next one was about flipping houses. She was pretty sure you had to buy a house before you flipped one. About halfway down the list of results, something caught her eye.

"NEED WORK RIGHT NOW? No experience" No references" No problem!"

She clicked on the link and was taken to a site called Task.um. It seemed to be listings of easy jobs for nominal pay. She put in her zip code and got a list of tasks people needed done in the area.

Moving, no. Bricklaying, no. Destroying a shed... could be fun, but they expected you to have your own tools and haul away what was left. Logo design... not really her thing. Then she found, "Need someone to buy and deliver a phone - prefer female." She clicked through, which required an annoying registration process. After a quick wardrobe change to business casual, she put her hair up into her trademark "power bun," and she was off to buy some lady a phone.

The job was simple enough. She picked up a pre-paid cellphone at the dollar store, for some reason the contact insisted she pay cash, and drove to an address in Johnston, a few blocks off Merle Hay Road. She parked on the street, in front of a typical suburban house with a big bay window. It seemed nicely kept for the residence of a shut-in. She walked up the the path to the house and knocked on the door. As she waited, she silently prayed the "prefer female" didn't mean she was about to get kidnapped, raped, and murdered. In her purse, she closed her hand around her pepper spray canister.

A tall, red-haired lady in full-blown dominatrix leathers answered the door, "Yes?"

Amy held up the phone. "Here you go. Your phone."

The lady smiled. "Thank you. You are a life saver. I broke my screen, and I've got back-to-back appointments today. I can't just run to the store dressed like this." She handed Amy a fifty dollar bill.

Amy imagined the woman would barely turn a head at Walmart, but she wasn't going to argue. Not bad. Twenty bucks profit for a half hour of work. If she did a few jobs like this every week, technically she could say she had a job. She'd be working almost every day, right?

The dominatrix started to close the door, but then she stopped and looked Amy up and down. "Say, you look like you might fit into some of my outfits. Are you into BDSM? Looking for work? I could use an apprentice. You could make a lot of money."

Amy quickly shook her head. "No!" Then she paused. "Wait, how much—No. Not my thing." She had no problem with the idea of punishing men, but the outfits weren't her style, and she found it kind of gross that they would get off on it. Besides, she'd have to send some kind of proof of employment to her father, and she doubted his heart could take it. For a guy who married a showgirl, he could be outright prudish when it came to his own daughter.

She turned and walked away quickly. When she heard the door close behind her, she glanced back in time to see the woman walk by the window, the phone in one hand and a complicated whip thing in the other. She was probably going to make her client activate the phone. That would be real torture.

In the car, she checked her phone for another job she could do on the way back. She found a job right away, but this one was a little strange. "Courier needed. Pick up paper sack at entrance of Ashby Park, handicapped parking. Deliver to this address..." The address and park were both near the route she was taking home, so she clicked through to accept the job.

Amy drove over to Ashby park. A rusty Toyota sat in one of the handicapped spaces, without a handicapped license plate or sign. Amy walked up and knocked on the window.

A big, greasy man sat in the driver's seat. He cranked down a manual window, and a smell like damp corn chips wafted from the car. "Sorry, honey. I'm not looking for a working girl."

It took Amy a minute to realize he thought she was a prostitute. She was wearing business casual, dammit. "I'm from Task Um. You're supposed to have a bag for me."

"Oh, yeah. I didn't expect a female." Weird, he said "female" exactly like that Nelson guy had. He reached behind his seat and pulled out a large, brown paper bag, stapled shut at the top.

"Thank you," Amy said. She turned and walked quickly to her car. Halfway there, however, she realized the smell was following her. She wasn't sure if the package smelled or if it had simply picked up the smell from the man's car. Just to be safe, she put the bag in her trunk.

She drove to a downtown address, a multi-floor office building inhabited by an insurance company. The

Task.um details for delivery were very specific, if a little odd. She turned left, ignoring the receptionist and headed for the stairwell. She climbed to the third floor, exited the stairwell, and looked at the men's room across the hall. She looked left, looked right, bit her lip, and dashed through the bathroom door.

She hadn't been thinking. She'd planned on stalls, like in a women's room. She was five steps in before she realized her mistakes, she turned, giving herself a perfect view down the row or urinals. There was a man standing at one. He looked over his shoulder and said, "Hello! I think you have the wrong bathroom."

Amy couldn't help gawking for a moment. Where she was standing, she had a perfect side view of his penis letting out a stream of urine. She'd never watched a man pee before—she wasn't some kind of pee-looker. And she'd never even seen one sober before. It was kind of fascinating in a disgusting sort of way.

"Sorry!" She turned away and felt her skin redden all the way from her cheeks to her toes. Why had they designed the bathroom to give a perfect view from the door?

Sure that her hair had turned red to the top of her bun, she hurried to the exit door and darted back in the stairwell.

The stairwell door was one of those steel affairs with the wire-reinforced glass window. Amy held back a bit and waited until she saw the man exit the restroom. Then she slunk forward through the restroom door again.

At least if she had to hang out in a men's restroom, this one seemed relatively clean and well-ventilated. She set the package in the back corner of the handicapped stall and hurried to the door.

She slid through the door just in time to run into the same man in the hallway. "Excuse me," she mumbled, and pushed past him into the staircase. He might have yelled something behind her, but with adrenaline pumping through her veins, it felt like she went down all three flights of stairs in six strides.

Once she was safely in her car, she checked the Task.um app and marked the job done. A message said that once the job was verified, twenty dollars would be transferred into her bank account. She preferred cash jobs, but money was money.

She realized she was trembling slightly. She wasn't used to going into strange office buildings, let alone their men's rooms. There was an oddly intrusive feel to it. Still, seeing a dick was easier than building a deck.

On the way back to her apartment, she stopped for gas. As usual, she untwisted the cap with the intention of putting it on top of her car, as her model lacked a convenient place to hang the cap and she'd broken the plastic tether. However, when she raised the cap, it caught on the intact plastic tether.

Amy froze. Had she somehow gotten in the wrong car? She tentatively looked in her back window. Those were definitely her cheap sunglasses, balled up tissues, and Diet Coke cans on the floor. She checked the license plate. It was her car, so she gassed it up. When the pump stopped, she tentatively picked up the cap by its tether, as if it might suddenly disappear. It didn't.

When she got home, she hung up her bras, put the rest of her clothes in the dryer, poured a drink, and started another load. She texted Patty so she wouldn't have to talk to her. "Found job. All good."

○ ○ ○

Andrew Jackson reversed his Corolla out of the handicapped spot and noticed the transmission was having a good day. He'd bought the car for $400 off a guy who'd rebuilt it as an educational project. It had come with a few spare parts including a bent-up set of Iowa license plates reading "PENYSBOY." A weird name to put on a car. Maybe the previous owner was a DJ.

With the money he was making, working these strange jobs for Task.um, he would soon be able to buy a much nicer car, one that would get females to notice him.

His phone beeped, and he eased the Corolla back into the space. Safety first. He checked his text message. "From TN: Your services are no longer needed. Sorry :)"

Andrew Jackson's car, the inexplicably named PENYSBOY, exploded in a ball of flame, scattering car parts, fast food wrappers, and pieces of Andrew Jackson, over Ashby Park.

○ ○ ○

Amy, having successfully adulted, doing laundry and making money in the same day, believed she needed a treat. Maybe she should get a good meal. Or maybe, she could go out to a club. She hadn't really expected to contact Holden again, but now she wondered if he was ready for some wingman duty.

She sent him a text while she was folding laundry. "u up for club?" Then she threw a few random emojis in just to make it interesting.

She unzipped her delicates bag and found two black bras, which was weird, as she was sure she'd only put one in. She checked them both for signs of super glue. They both had wires glued in.

As she was staring at the bras suspiciously, her phone buzzed. "Can't working late. Guy in ashby park blew himself" A moment later, a second message came in. "Up. Blew himself up."

She replied. "Sux. I was just there. Glad I wasn't exploded."

So, with nothing else to do, Amy actually looked at Task.um. There, she saw a job even stranger than the last, and depending on the cost of motor oil, a task that would net her $40. Fifteen minutes later, she was in the dollar store buying a liter bottle of Diet Coke and a bottle of motor oil.

"You don't want that," the clerk said.

"What?" Amy asked.

"I shouldn't say this, but the oil here sucks. There's an auto parts place like a block that way." He pointed.

Amy shrugged. "Yeah, but they don't have diet coke, and it's not going in my car."

"Suit yourself."

She paid and took the bottles out to the parking lot. Not wanting to be wasteful, she took a deep drink of the Coke before dumping the remainder out on the parking lot. Then she started the slow and messy job of pouring the oil into the bottle. After 30 seconds of trying, she went back to the dollar store and bought paper towels and a funnel—two dollars removed from her profit margin. She tried not to make eye contact with the clerk. She didn't imagine the clerk knew what she was doing—she didn't really know that herself—but he would no doubt imagine something even stranger.

She went back to her car, finished pouring the oil, and cleaned up the soda bottle. She threw the used paper towels and the empty oil bottle into the cheap plastic bag from the dollar store and tied it tight.

Why the hell was someone paying her to leave a soda bottle full of motor oil downtown? If someone was simply out of oil, they're probably prefer it in the proper container and with no Diet Coke residue. Her GPS led her to the address, and she found a parking space nearby—it was a weeknight in a residential neighborhood, a swanky one at that.

She set the bottle next to a lamppost as instructed and drove down the hill, across Grande Ave to a Mexican place she'd seen earlier, boasting thirty-ounce margaritas.

30

After many margaritas, she took an Uber home. The driver insisted on helping her up to her apartment, which made her nervous as hell. She tried her keys, but they didn't want to slide into the lock, and even after she forced them in, they refused to turn. She checked the number on the door, apartment five. It was her apartment.

After a few minutes trying to turn the keys, the door opened suddenly, ripping the keys from her hands. Standing in the doorway was her was her neighbor, Mrs. Ochmonek.

Amy tried to give her a friendly smile. "Good evening, Mrs. Ochmoney Mrs. Ochmaaaa. Mrs... Raquel. I... Um, why are you in my apartment?"

From the living room, she heard Raquel's husband, Jake, yell, "Raquel, what is it?"

"Just the neighbor girl. She's got a guy with her." She turned back around and smiled at them.

"What the fuck are you doing in my apartment?" Amy blurted out.

Raquel pointed to the number on the door. "No sweetie. Jack and I live in five. You live in six. Are you okay?"

She wanted to argue more, but she was very tired, and she had an Uber driver to dispose of. She pointed at the man, "Sorry, Raquel, this is Ed. He was my Uber driver. He's just leaving." She said the last bit with a bit of emphasis, like maybe she'd come to the wrong door on purpose.

Raquel gave her a meaningful look. Then she smiled to the driver. "Thank you, Ed. I can handle it from here."

"Okay, have a good night," Ed said, hurrying to the stairs and disappearing.

"Thanks. I don't know if he was a creeper, but I didn't want to take a chance," she said, acting as if it was a calculated plan to try opening the wrong door.

Raquel retrieved her keys from the door and took hold of Amy's shoulders, steering her across the hall.

"You never worry about bothering us if you need anything, dear."

Amy tried to get her keys in the apartment six lock, they turned smoothly, but she still felt turned around. The hallway was gently spinning around her, so that might have accounted for the feeling, but how had she misremembered her apartment number? "God as my witness," Amy said, "I will never drink tequila ever again." She finally slammed the keys home and got her door open.

"Of course, you won't, sweetie. Now go lie down." Raquel backed out shutting the door behind her.

Amy blinked at the apartment. The floor plan was a mirror image of the one she'd lived in for three years, and yet it contained all her stuff. She wandered over to the bed. All she wanted to do was get under the covers and deal with it in the morning. However, all the furniture was in the wrong place, and she was dizzy. Her muscle memory betrayed her. She missed the bed and fell on the floor.

○ ○ ○

David Graves didn't like working late. It annoyed his girlfriend, Raven. However, it was her father, who was also his boss, who had asked him to stay. This wouldn't have been so bad if he had lots to do, but in his average eight-hour day, he generally did about two hours' worth of paperwork and fired a few people.

He could have left two hours ago, if not for this meeting. Two hours wasn't quite long enough to go home and take a nap, and he'd done all his firings for the day. He could practice his dark wizardry, but he was still new, and the last time he'd done that without someone to guide him, he'd set the closest Dairy Queen on fire, which meant no more Mister Misty Freezes or Dilly Bars unless he wanted to drive all the way across town.

Too late to act on it, he realized going for a Mister Misty Freeze would have been a great way to kill an hour. He wished he'd thought of it earlier.

Bored, David looked up some Satanic Subreddits and forums he sometimes perused for the fun of it. Usually, they were clueless, but today, one of them had linked to a BuzzPage article about the celebrity computer guy Tommy Norman. Since selling his company to Intel five years ago, the guy had gotten into some sketchy stuff, but the headline of the article had gotten it put in the forum. "Tommy Norman Says NSA Worships Satan."

As far as David knew, he was right. There were several government agencies who had been infiltrated by their people, the higher profile the better. Though oddly, they claimed not to have anyone at the IRS.

Fifteen minutes after he was due, Charlie Stevens walked through David's door. "David, good to see you again. How's my little girl doing?"

David neglected to tell Charlie that his "little girl" had punched David hard enough two nights ago to knock him out cold. He didn't even remember why anymore—probably because one of her customers had pissed her off. "She's doing great, Charlie."

"Wonderful. I don't suppose you've gotten her pregnant yet..."

David shook his head. "No, I'm afraid not." Apparently, there was some kind of prophecy involving their marriage. It might just involve the end of the world. The possibility of conceiving the Antichrist gave them a little extra reason to be careful about birth control. Lately, however, that hadn't been much of a concern, as they were going through a rough patch. They weren't even sleeping in the same bed most nights.

"Well, keep trying." David internally braced himself, but fortunately, Charlie wasn't going to offer any detailed sexual advice today. "So, I guess you know why I've asked you to stay late today."

"Does it involve the problem with the computers?"

Charlie nodded. "That is the most important item of the day. We have to keep sending our quota of souls to Hell."

"How?" David asked, having no ideas of his own.

"Good question, Son. I think we're going to have to go old-school. Chanting to open a portal and then using the dagger to take souls directly instead of just downloading them in."

"You mean... You want me to stab people in the heart with the big dagger?"

Charlie shrugged. "I don't know of a better way to do it. So, I'm going to need you to kidnap Randy Clarke so we can sacrifice him during our next meeting. And then we can start planning to officially make you my son-in-law and take over as president of the company."

"Well, I... That sounds great Charlie." That did *not* sound great at all. It was bad enough David had to kill his predecessor to get his current job. He didn't want to murder Randy Clarke too. "But shouldn't you give Randy a second chance?"

"Not unless he can find someone who can fix that software. He'd never be able to manage that."

"I've heard he's already found someone who can do it," David said. "He's been thinking about talking to Tommy Norman." The name was fresh in his mind after reading that article.

This took Charlie by surprise. "That just might work. Apparently when he was still doing consulting, he did some work for us in one of the spy agencies—"

"The NSA," David supplied.

"He even apparently turned a couple angels, got dirt on them."

"I didn't know angels had dirt to get." Another thought struck him. "The NSA keeps tabs on angels?"

"Apparently, they do." Charlie shrugged. "And people think government can't accomplish anything. But why would Norman come here? The last I checked, he was down in Bolivia snorting piles of cocaine and bang-ing hookers. He's already got more money than he

ing hookers. He's already got more money than he could ever spend."

Inspiration struck David in that moment. He could see it all in his head. "What if we gave him a taste of the MediaStorm money? I bet he'd pull himself off a couple hookers for a stack of money that large."

Charlie nodded. "I think you're onto something. I'll call up our people in the State Department, make sure he doesn't have any charges against him in any countries we extradite to. But keep Randy's hands off this, David. I want you to head this one up. You've convinced me not to kill Randy outright, but I'm thinking of scaling back his role for the time being, and I think it's time for you to be involved in something larger."

Making a face, David said, "Are you sure I'm the right guy for this kind of job?"

Looking him straight in the eyes, Charlie said, "I know for a fact you're not. When our Evil Lord handed out gifts, he enhanced your muscles and good looks. He must have known you could have used a functioning brain, but he didn't bother to try."

David felt rather insulted by this. He was a college graduate. Maybe the Evil Lord thought he was smart enough.

"I'm pretty sure that as Matt Rose's protégé the dark lord meant for you to be a leg-breaker. However, you happen to be dating my girl, and right now, I'm not giving any additional responsibility to Randy."

○ ○ ○

Amy walked into a Polk County government building, a bland concrete structure full of administrative offices, wondering if she'd taken one Task.um job she should have left alone.

Most of her jobs were mundane. For two days, she'd worked as a receptionist for a company that sold hose clamps. She'd helped a hardware store disassemble some metal shelving. She'd even spent half day hauling wheelbarrows of mulch for a landscaping company. She enjoyed the variety.

However, the stranger jobs tended to be easier, higher-paying jobs, and they usually dealt in cash rather than going through the Task.um repayment system, which could hold money for seventy-two hours. She had worked for them a full week now, and she'd forwarded her first earning statement, $539 after taxes, to her father and Debbie to peruse just this morning.

So, here she was wandering the halls of a giant cement building, doing her most profitable job yet, $140 cash for an hour of work. She was supposed to take a paper bag to a man in a Chicago Bears jacket. She'd gotten the bag at Burger King by asking for McDonald's special sauce on a Whopper when she went through the drive through. The guy hadn't challenged her on it. He hadn't even asked her to pay, and it was a plain, brown bag, not a Burger King bag. She kind of wished he would have thrown in a Whopper, as she hadn't eaten yet.

The paper bag was suspiciously heavy, and when the man at the window handed it to her, one of the other employees had yelled, "Danny, are you selling drugs again?" She really hoped it wasn't drugs. Drugs made her nervous, and she'd had to deal with them enough in college. Her roommate had gotten hooked on meth and blamed it on Amy moping around the room.

Part of the government building was an art gallery, supposedly celebrating Polk County in all its diversity. She decided to take a look. However, she had trouble focusing on the artwork. Not only was she on the lookout for a Bears jacket, but her mind kept going back to two identical black bras, with glue in the same place.

Sure, her apartment moving across the hall should have bothered her more—it was hell finding the bathroom in the dark—but that was just a memory change. She physically possessed two super-glued black bras. She'd finally worked up the courage to examine them, and they even fit the same. Today, she'd worn one of them, and every time she moved, the rough, glued area scraped across her skin. She vowed to throw out both and use the money from this job to buy replacements.

On the other end of the gallery, she spotted a man in the Bears jacket, a thick-set guy with a big mustache and glasses. She approached him and said, "You forgot your lunch again." It was a sort-of code. She was pretty sure the bag didn't contain anything lunch-like.

As he took the bag, the man discretely slipped her a folded stack of crisp twenty-dollar bills, and she noticed he was wearing clear latex gloves. Maybe he had a germ issue like that millionaire guy from that movie, *The Aviator.*

He pointed to the display he was looking at, a piece of Astroturf painted red. "Does that look like art to you?"

Amy shrugged. "It has a little card by it, so sure. I guess."

She turned and hurried out of the sterile government building into the warm spring day. She was wearing a tight, black sweater, a bit heavy for the weather, but it looked good on her, and she didn't mind suffering a bit for fashion.

Once she had the AC going, she sat in her car and checked her phone. There was an open job coming up in the next five minutes, and she wouldn't even have to drive. All she had to do was pick up someone in front of the building where she was parked and drive them wherever they wanted. She thought it was kind of weird that they'd do it on Task.um instead of just calling for an Uber. But if they wanted to waste money, that was none of her business. After waiting ten minutes, she drove around to the front of the building and waited.

The guy with the mustache and Bears jacket burst through the front door, moving fast for a big guy. He was bleeding from a wound to his shoulder. Before he got in the car, he whipped off the Bears jacket and turned it inside out, so it now looked like a plain, blue jacket. That must have hurt like hell with his shoulder wound.

Before Amy could assimilate what was going on, the guy jumped in her car and yelled, "Drive!" He still had the paper bag in his hand.

She just stared at him for a second. "You're bleeding on my seats." She was a little in shock and couldn't think to do anything else.

"Go! The sooner you go, the quicker I'll stop bleeding on your seats."

She was still having trouble with what was going on. "Where?"

"You really need to leave now. Just drive away from here."

She sighed and rolled her eyes, tired of asking the same question and getting no answer. "Okay, whatever."

She pulled onto the street and drove a couple of blocks, only slowing down once for a police car going the other way. As soon as she'd started driving, the guy had gotten on his phone. He gave her an address.

"Did someone shoot you?" she asked, trying to keep her eyes on the road and type the address into her phone at the same time.

He shook his head emphatically. "No, just popped a giant zit. You know how it is you get a really big zit, and it pops at the worst time."

The blood hadn't bothered her, but the mention of popping made her empty stomach roll. She shook her head. "No, I wouldn't. Not like that. "You might need medical attention."

He glanced at her again. "Weren't you the girl who delivered my... package inside? I thought they'd get me someone else to be a driver."

"I'm with Task Um. It's a service. Like GrubHub or Uber."

"And you bring people unmarked packages?"

"I guess so. Sometimes. The jobs are kind of flexible. I picked the first one because it was easy and paid well. I just took the driving gig because I was already outside the pickup address." She was babbling, still a little in shock at a guy bleeding in her car.

He looked over at her. "I can't believe they hired a random person on the Internet to be my backup." He sounded pretty unhappy, but she supposed it was his prerogative to be a little grumpy. He was oozing blood. "How old are you, anyway?"

"I'm twenty-five." She took a ramp onto I-235 and headed Northeast across the Des Moines River. The work "backup" floated through her head. He was some kind of criminal, and she was his backup, and accessory to whatever crime he'd just committed. This was no fucking good.

When they were partway across the river, he used his good arm to take off his glasses, pull off his mustache, and dump them both in the paper bag. "Can you get in the right lane?" He rolled down the window, and as soon as she was in the outer lane, he threw the bag out the window, where it sailed over the side of the bridge, presumably to land in the river.

"So, where are we going?"

"I need a doctor."

"That's fucking obvious." As his driver, she felt a responsibility to make small talk. "Um, so are you from around here?"

"I'd rather not answer that."

"Okay..." She tried again. "Going to be in town long?

"How about we call that none of your fucking business?"

For a few weeks last year, Amy had worked for a ride-sharing startup, a Des Moines-based wannabe Uber-killer that no longer existed. She'd been hired to work in the office, but she went out a few times when they needed drivers. So being treated like this wasn't too out of the ordinary. She nodded. "No problem there. I'm just going to keep my eyes on the road. Looking straight ahead, so I wouldn't even be able to pick you out of a line-up, Mr...?"

"You're telling me you can't pick me out of a line-up and you're asking for my *name?* That's a special kind of crazy." He thought for a moment. "If you have to call me something, call me Barney. Like the dinosaur. My kid loves him."

"Sorry. I guess I'm a little flustered. I don't spend a lot of time hanging out with... people with such serious acne." She took an offramp, put on her blinker and waited to take a left turn.

His voice softened. "Oh, don't worry. You're doing great, Honey."

Amy wanted to tell him not to call her Honey, but he seemed to be some sort of criminal or maniac, so she let it drop. "I guess I'm just trying to be nice. We do that in Iowa."

"What makes you think I'm not from Iowa?"

She shrugged. "How about a blue and orange Bears jacket and the thick Chicago accent? Together, they are pretty conspicuous." She stopped the car in front of a shady-looking animal clinic. "Okay, I guess this is it."

"They'll want you to pull around back."

As she parked the car for the second time, she asked, "Seriously though, you did something bad back there, didn't you? Am I an accessory in a crime now?"

"Stop asking me questions," he said. "Plausible deniability." He gave her an appraising look. "You don't seem too upset about all this, kid."

"Partly, I'm still processing." She shrugged. "Besides, I'd rather do this than be a farm wife."

The guy turned to her and asked, "Is that something that might happen, like *accidentally?*"

She shrugged, "You never know. It happened to most of the girls in my high school class."

The big man guffawed. "I like you, kid." He pulled a stack of money and a card from his wallet and placed it all on the dashboard. "This is for the ride, plus the number of a guy I know who can set you up with some higher paying jobs." He added two hundred-dollar bills to the pile. "And that's for staying cool. You'll want to steam-clean those seats right away. They'll stain if you don't."

"I know. I've done ride sharing before. And thanks." She didn't know whether the thanks was sarcastic or not. She didn't like the idea of needing to clean his blood out of her car, but he'd paid her a lot.

Later at the car wash, as she was thoroughly shampooing the blood out of her car, she overheard the radio of the guy at the vacuum next to her. The police were on the lookout for a heavyset man, glasses and a thick mustache, last seen wearing a Chicago Bears jacket. He'd just assassinated the assistant to the Polk County Treasurer.

Amy drove herself home, crawled into her nest of a bed, and started to shake. What was it all about—deliveries to professional sadists, motor oil in pop bottles, leaving things in toilet stalls, and now assassination? She was beginning to believe Task.um was not a safe company to work for, which would explain why it paid so much and so often her jobs paid cash. When she felt calm enough, she made herself a giant rum and Diet Coke.

3

Macing Angels

Twenty-Six Years Ago...

Michael Love sat alone in the hospital room and gazed at the tiny girl in the incubator. A week ago, he'd lost his wife Sarah in childbirth. He'd gone through all the motions, notified relatives, bought a pair of cemetery plots, made arrangements, sat through the funeral, but none of it felt real. Every moment he wasn't taking care of those arrangements, he'd been right here, looking at the tiny baby, undersized, sickly, his little girl.

He kept trying to tell himself that he was a good person. He'd done nothing that could have caused this. For a lawyer, he thought he'd been a pretty good guy. He didn't represent gang bangers or murderers; he wrote wills and transferred property. The worst he'd done is get Clarence Walton, the local undertaker, out of a DUI by claiming the old drunk was accidentally high on embalming fluid.

However, he couldn't help but think his baby's poor condition must be some fault of his, a sanction for some moral failing. Why would God punish him like this—taking his wife, giving him an undersized baby with a life-threatening infection? What had he done to deserve this?

He watched the tiny chest rise and fall. That and the beeping machines were the only reason he knew she was alive, his little America Mustang. Such a big name for such a tiny girl. He'd loved Sarah so much, but now he had a daughter, and he needed to be pragmatic. A girl needed a mother. Maybe he could even find a woman with a little girl of her own, a big sister for America.

Michael lowered his head and did something he hadn't done since he was a little boy. He prayed, with all his heart and soul. "Lord, please, protect this tiny child. If she lives, I promise to teach her to be a good Christian." He felt like he needed to do something to sweeten the deal, like promise she would become a nun, but he wasn't Catholic. Also being an attorney, he was sensitive to over-promising on the terms of a contract. "I promise to raise her to serve you as a holy warrior to fight for your glory." There, that language was subservient but suitably vague.

Someone knocked on the door softly, and he said, "Yes," nearly as softly, expecting it to be a nurse or one of the doctors.

The door opened, and a man walked in. He didn't look like a doctor. In fact, he reminded Michael of most of the judges he worked with, heavyset, going a little bald, and wearing a suit.

Michael glared at the newcomer. "Who the hell are you?"

○ ○ ○

Way too early for normal people, Amy's phone rang. Her head felt like it would split down the middle, but she answered it to save herself from listening to her ringtone. "Yeah?" she said with neither enthusiasm nor encouragement. "What?"

"If that's the attitude you're going to have, I can hang up right now." It was Debbie, the evil stepsister.

"Oh, hello, Debbie. How are you today?" Amy put in a ten percent attempt to sound friendly and perky, but she knew she was incapable of carrying it off so early and so hung over.

"Well, Mom asked me to do you a favor and get you a job. But if you aren't interested..."

Amy only took a second to answer. "What? Why? I already have a job."

Debbie didn't sigh, but Amy was sure she was holding it in. "Mom says your current job isn't good enough. There's no benefits and no regular hours. You're basically just doing spot jobs for a website."

"What the fuck does that matter? I'm working."

"Please, Amy, don't curse. She thinks you should have a better job, and Daddy agrees."

"Of course Daddy agrees. Your mother didn't have any trouble with me making tacos or working in a coffee shop. I didn't get benefits or regular hours there."

"I'm not arguing semantics with you, Amy. I'm just passing on the message. Your little gig economy website—"

"Task Um. It is a real job. In fact, yesterday felt more real than any day working in food service."

"Whatever. Your little website is not a good enough employer. You need to find a better job."

Amy hadn't planned to go back to work for Task.um today anyway. Not only was she hung over, but despite the amount of rum she'd consumed last night, she could clearly remember steam cleaning blood out of her car. Part of her was stubborn enough to want to argue the point, but she supposed it didn't hurt to ask. "So, what's the job?"

"I'm not really sure, but Tommy Norman's been giving some business to our firm lately. We're helping him set up some office space for Norman, LLC."

"Tommy Norman? I thought he was on the run from the IRS. Didn't he try to start a civil war in Bolivia?"

"Ha. Ha. Hah!" Debbie gave Amy her fake laugh. "All those charges were dropped. Just a simple error on Mr. Norman's tax bill. And that whole thing in Bolivia was just a misunderstanding with a couple of heavily armed local farmers. You grew up around farmers. You know how stubborn they can be."

"I know there's a big difference between Bolivia and Holstein. Are you sure those local farmers weren't a couple drug lords? Isn't cocaine, like, their only agricultural export?"

"I have no idea what you're talking about."

Amy sighed. If she wanted to stay in Des Moines rent free, she really did need a job her father approved of. She wasn't crazy about working for one of the world's most notable loonies, but he was often at odds with the US government. How often could he really be in Des Moines? "Okay, but I won't be a drug mule."

"I'm sure that won't be a problem. Just to be safe, you might want to include that in your cover letter, about not being a drug mule. Just in case." Debbie was rambling. That was probably a bad sign.

"You want me to write a cover letter? I take it I'm not going to be the janitor then? Most of my jobs just have an online application. I've done so many now, my phone autofills the forms. Though, it sometimes puts my birth date as the second line of my mailing address."

"Just make up a resumé and write a cover letter. It isn't hard. Look up instructions on the Internet or something."

"Okay, but you know I don't have a regular computer, just my phone."

"Don't they have all those things at the library? You're not allergic to the library, are you?"

"No." She just didn't care to sit around with a bunch of guys pretending not to look at porn and getting themselves worked up. They'd probably think she was there for a hookup. The last time she'd used a library computer, a guy had followed her to the parking lot and asked her to show him her tits.

"You act like you can't possibly be bothered to solve the simplest problems. This is why you didn't get your paralegal certificate. You job shadowed Dad as soon as you were old enough to walk. You used to do his correspondence. You could pass the bar right now if you had the academic credentials. Yet somehow you didn't graduate community college. You're just lazy."

Amy rolled her eyes with such resolve, she was afraid she might sprain something. She found it amazing how much Debbie could sound like her mother, like criticism was in their DNA. "I'm sure you're right, Debbie."

"Oh, and do you have an interview suit?"

"Yes. You know I have nice clothes."

"I just wanted to make sure you hadn't pawned them for cheap wine or whatever it is you do."

Amy rolled her eyes a second time. Yes, she liked a drink or two, but Debbie knew Dad paid the credit cards. It wasn't the most dignified situation, but slightly more so than pawning her clothes. "Goodbye now, Debbie." She hung up.

After a moment of thought, Amy decided that working for Tommy Norman was a horrible idea, especially if he had business with Debbie. She spent the rest of the day binge watching cheesy, girly movies on the Lifemark Channel app.

Around six, she decided she needed food and drink. Whenever she decided to quit a job, she made it a habit to spend a couple days celebrating. She sent a text to Holden. "What you doing? Food?"

Holden texted back. "Just going out with friends. Want to tag along?"

Amy considered that for a moment. She didn't think Holden had a lot of friends in town yet. Maybe he just made friends easily, unlike Amy who only had a long line of work friends she didn't work with anymore, college friends who moved on to start families, and high-school friends who she had almost nothing in common with anymore.

She replied to Holden's text. "Sure."

○ ○ ○

Amy had never been to Paddy's Barn and Grill. The building looked like it was literally an old barn, but the conversion had been quite thorough. Pushing open a large, modern door revealed a dark interior. Looking around as she let her eyes adjust to the lighting, she found Holden waving at her from a tall table of guys in a back corner. She walked over and hopped up into a chair. "Hi, I'm Amy, Holden's friend."

A big guy in his mid-fifties, apparently the alpha of the group, pointed at his chest with his thumb. "Elliot." He pointed to guys around the table, and Amy tried to remember a detail about each of them to match the name. "Seth..." Bald guy, mustache. "Seth's partner, Howard..." Dark hair, sharp features.

Amy nodded. "Partners, that's cool. How long have you two been together?"

"Three years," Howard answered.

Elliot continued the introductions. "Johnathon..." A short haircut that still showed a bit of natural curl. "And Mark." Curly hair, glasses, looked like an accountant. "You know Holden, of course." Holden was definitely the baby of the group, the only one in his twenties.

Amy nodded. "Cool. Hi, everybody." She'd never hung out with a whole table of gay guys before. There probably weren't that many gay guys in the town she

48

grew up in. Well, statistically, there probably were, but they were firmly in the closet.

Mark had been in the middle of a story when she showed up, and now she was settled, he continued. "So, the wife is sleeping with everyone in the trailer park. The husband finds out about it, and he decides he's going to burn down everyone's trailers. Of course, he's heavily intoxicated and naked..."

"They're always naked," Howard confirmed.

Everyone around the table nodded, as if this was an everyday occurrence.

"He proceeds to get more gasoline on himself than on his neighbor's trailer..." He paused and turned to Amy. "I hope this isn't making you uncomfortable."

Amy shrugged. "No, I'm cool."

He continued to talk to Amy. "Just for context, gasoline doesn't burn in real life like it does in the movies. It doesn't follow a nice, tidy path. It's the fumes that actually explode. So, if you're ever covered in gasoline, the last thing you want to do is get anywhere near open flame."

Amy nodded. "Seems like a good idea even if gasoline did behave like it does in the movies."

Mark nodded. "Right? So, this guy lights a match to throw at his buddy's trailer, and he explodes."

"I bet he felt stupid," Amy said.

Mark shook his head. "Oh, no. He died."

They shared a moment of silence, only broken when a waitress came by. Elliot ordered them a round. Amy ordered a rum and Diet Coke. As Elliot got out his wallet to tip the waitress, Amy noticed his wallet contained a badge. Suddenly, Mark's story made more sense. These weren't Holden's new gay friends. They were his new cop friends.

While they waited for their drinks, Elliot said, "Okay, I got a weird one. My buddy on the Capitol Police gave me a call. Someone dumped motor oil all over the driveway of the governor's mansion."

Amy felt her cheeks heat. She'd transported the motor oil to that neighborhood in a Diet Coke bottle. She hadn't known why. She still didn't know why.

"Holy shit," Johnathon said. "What happened?"

"Well, you know that driveway has a bit of a slope, and the troopers they assign to drive her are always going too fast. Her official SUV slid across the street and hopped onto the lawn of a homeowner, tearing up the grass and demolishing a fountain. And you know all the homeowners in that neighborhood are loaded, even if the governor wasn't involved. They shut down the household and questioned people, the trooper driving her has a broken nose from the airbag, and madam governor's schedule had to be pushed back a full day. The only clue they found was a Diet Coke bottle full of oil residue in a dumpster down the street."

Howard shook his head. "Freaking weird, man. Why did they put the oil in a coke bottle?"

Elliot shrugged. "Beats me. Maybe they were trying to confuse us. If that was their goal, it worked."

"Well," Holden said, "some people aren't that hard to confuse."

Elliot snorted and the joke and flipped him the bird. "Up yours, rookie."

They got their drinks, and Amy immediately drained half of hers. She couldn't believe what she was hearing. Her little job distributing motor oil had been some kind of attack on the governor. She was definitely not going back to Task.um.

Elliot shrugged. "Maybe we'll never know why it happened."

Seth and Mark both talked about their weeks, which seemed like pretty typical cop stuff to Amy. Then Elliot asked, "So, you've been pretty quiet, Howard, what's up with you?"

Howard had one of those really deep voices that Amy associated with preachers or soul artists like Isaac Hayes. "Well, you know, I've been filling in for Detective Meyer, she's still on maternity leave. The detectives have me doing leg work on this whole deal with the assistant county treasurer."

Amy's shoulders were so tight her back started to ache. She downed the rest of her drink.

"I've been asking basic questions of family, friends, coworkers, and not one of them has a clue why an outside hitter, a mob hitter no less, might be after an Iowa bureaucrat. The guy used some kind of Internet temp agency for the getaway driver and weapon purchase. We can see the jobs, we can see that they were taken by someone, but we don't even know who worked them. The company's based in Bolivia, the domain is registered in Umeccistan, and they're not looking to give up lots of information to local police departments in the US."

"But you know who did it?" Amy asked. She felt bad. She probably could help if she just spoke up, but she didn't want to incriminate herself. "You said it was a mob hit?"

Howard shrugged. "That's the working theory based on methods. The guy was at least a professional. He walked in cool as a cucumber, wearing just enough disguise to throw off casual observers, and shot without hesitation or worry about collateral damage. Then he disappeared. Some witnesses saw him get into a silver Honda Civic, so no luck there as there's over a thousand of those in Polk County. He probably tossed the murder weapon and disguise in a dumpster or in the river, but he did it far enough outside our search perimeter we never found it."

The waitress brought a second round and Holden paid for it. Amy took another slug from her fresh rum and coke.

Seth spoke up, saying, "You guys complaining about your assignments. The biggest investigation I've been involved with this week is a woman loitering in a men's room downtown."

Amy choked on her drink. Holden patted her on the back a couple times.

"You okay?" Holden asked.

Amy nodded. "Yeah, just went down the wrong pipe."

"How's work been treating you?" he asked.

Amy returned a nervous smile as six policemen turned to look at her, half of which she could assist in their casework based on how her job had been going.

"Oh, I'm going to quit."

"Amy!" Holden said. "I just met this girl a week ago, and she'd just ended a job. Now you're quitting again?"

She shrugged. "What can I say? It wasn't agreeing with me. Besides, it's..." She didn't want to name Task.um, as Howard was currently investigating it. "There's not really a set schedule. I'm not going to quit so much as drop off the face of the Earth as far as they're concerned. Besides, my stepsister, Debbie, has something lined up for me." She hadn't intended to add that last part, but she didn't want to sound like so much of a loser.

"Oh," Holden said. "That's great. What would you be doing?"

She shrugged. "I don't know. I'll just be working with some company that uses her law firm. Debbie is a Senior Associate at Nelson and Healey." She figured it was better not to mention Tommy Norman by name, just in case there were any warrants out for him.

"Oh, shit," Mark said, "Your sister is Debbie Sutter?"

"Stepsister, but yes."

Mark continued. "She represented a guy I picked up on drug charges, the guy had five grams of cocaine on him. She got him off, convinced a judge he'd just found it at the bar. He was 'trying to keep it out of the hands of kids.' Which I'm sure he would have. There were no kids up his nose."

Embarrassed, Amy shrugged. "Well, you can't pick your stepsister. I'm still mad at my dad for marrying her mom, and that was twenty-five years ago."

This provoked a laugh from the officers, even Mark. "I'm just giving you crap, Amy. I know you can't help that your stepsister's a shark."

"Seriously, though," Amy said. "I'd rather not work for one of Debbie's clients. I'm kind of on the fence. I'm sure, just like most of my jobs, I'll last about a week before I quit or they fire me."

Amy sighed and finished another rum and Diet Coke.

"Still," she continued, "the best thing I ever did was get away from Calltelestar Peopleconnect. My boss there was this guy named David Graves. I think he was the most evil human being I've ever met."

The guys continued to tell cop stories into the night, and Amy was pleased to find she was not at all responsible for the majority of them, after a somewhat bad start. She ended up telling her bra story.

Seth offered, "That sounds like one of those Mandela Effects."

She raised an eyebrow. "Isn't that like a dead African guy? You think he somehow duplicated my bra?"

He shook his head. "No, it's just this Internet thing, where people think reality is being changed, but only some people are noticing. The first big one was whether or not Nelson Mandela died in prison."

"Like how some people think Bubba Strayhorn is alive, and some people think he's dead?"

"Exactly," Seth nodded.

At the end of the night, Holden took Amy home in her car and put her to bed. She gave him a big hug for this. "You're such a good boy, Holden. You're, like, my best friend now, you know."

He grinned. "Thank you, Amy. I think you're pretty awesome too."

"Your cop friends are pretty cool. I thought all cops were assholes."

"Well Amy, there are all kinds of cops. Let's just say they ones that would be try to make friends with a

gay, Latino rookie are the kind that don't fit that stereo-
type."

Once Holden was gone, she put on her pajamas, a
pair of shorts and a tank-top, and went to sleep.

○ ○ ○

Across town, David Graves handed an envelope
containing $5000 to a mortician. "You're sure this isn't
traceable?" he asked the mortician.

The mortician shrugged. "Maybe someone has his
DNA in their system, but if the police do figure out who
owned the foot, they're going to find a gangster that's
still supposed to be alive. Officially, Eddy did not come
through my facility."

Graves nodded and took the package. "All right."

"If you don't mind," the mortician paused. "Why
do you need a human foot?"

David sighed. "My neighbor's been having a lot of
late-night parties. I've talked to him about the noise,
but he won't listen."

The mortician nodded but looked confused.

Later that night, David buried the foot in his neighbor's prize rose garden. Tomorrow, the police would
get an anonymous tip. After that, he anticipated his
neighbor would be less popular.

David sighed. He knew he'd sold his soul, and he
was supposed to be evil and everything, and part of
that meant doing evil deeds and punishing those who
crossed him in the most severe manner imaginable.
Sometimes, though, it just seemed like a lot of trouble.

○ ○ ○

That night, Ottoel, an angel of the Lord, appeared
in Amy's bedroom.

The apartment was dark, so Ottoel turned on the
overhead light, and said in a deep voice, not unlike one
used by a preacher or soul artists like Isaac Hayes, "I
am Ottoel, an angel of the Lord, and you..." He looked

down at the bed and found only a pile of covers, snoring softly.

Inching forward, Ottoel grabbed a corner of the duvet cover and pulled it down to Amy's waist, to show her tank top had turned sideways, and her left boob was hanging out the arm hole.

Ottoel covered his eyes, not sure if he was supposed to see something like that. He knew for sure there was a prohibition against angels mating with human women, and although he didn't think it was written down anywhere, spying on them in their bedrooms was, at the very least, frowned upon. He inched forward, blocking Amy's offending nipple from his view, grabbed the edge of her Duvet, and then pulled it up to her neck. Now he should be able to introduce himself...

"Excuse me," Amy asked, straightening her tank top under the duvet. "What are you doing in my bedroom?" She grabbed her purse and started fishing through it. "My best friend's a cop. You better leave right now."

Ottoel had expected her to cower in fear or start screaming. However, she seemed quite calm. "Um..." Ottoel said, "I am an angel of the Lord?" He made it sound like a question. Stupid. He cleared his throat and tried again in the big angel voice.

"I am Ottoel, an angel of the Lord. I have come to you, with a task from the Almighty."

"What?" Amy held up a finger. "Hold that thought for a second. Oh, there it is..."

Ottoel sighed. "Whatever. Look, it's simple. I am an angel of the Lord, sent here to—" A blast of foaming pepper spray hit him square in the face, and he gagged.

"Oh Lord!" he yelled. The burning was so severe, he clutched his hands to his face and unfurled his wings to block any other incoming alchemical fire.

"Holy shit!" Amy screamed.

4

Meeting with Notable Sociopaths

Amy was shocked, to put it lightly. At first, she had tried to stay as calm as possible and considered herself lucky that the man—*creature?—*had given her time to locate her pepper spray. Now she was regretted not hearing him out. But still, sneaking up on people while they slept was inconsiderate. The angel was lucky she didn't keep a gun in her purse. Of course, angels might be bullet proof. Although, they seemed susceptible enough to pepper spray.

Ottoel certainly hadn't looked like an angel. He looked like a chubby, fatherly man wearing an antique suit and hat. He reminded Amy of one of the rural judges her dad was always hanging out with. The wings had changed her mind though.

Her brain was having trouble fully engaging. She wondered whether she should follow through with calling Holden or assist what seemed to be an authentic holy creature. Because it did, in fact, seem she had encountered a bona fide angel, she decided not to call Holden. What could he do? He wasn't in the church police.

She suffered a brief coughing fit. The pepper spray she'd used was foaming and not supposed to harm the user, but it most definitely was hanging in the air. She walked over and opened all the windows.

Maybe, just to be careful, she should zip-tie the angel's hands together, giving her time to decide on a better course of action. Wasn't that what they did on TV shows, zip-tie people's hands together? Or did they have those plastic cuffs like Holden used?

There were two problems with the zip tie plan. First, the angel-creature was clutching its hands to its eyes, somewhere behind the huge wings. Second, she probably didn't have any zip-ties, or duct tape, or electrical tape, being neither into DIY nor kinky stuff.

She abandoned the captivity idea and decided to go with questioning instead. After all, she still had the pepper spray, and the creature had unfurled a giant pair of wings, which lent credence to the angel story.

"Um, Angel?" she asked.

"Ottoel," came the creature's timid response. It seemed to be in genuine pain, and she was sort of starting to feel sorry for it.

"Otto-L?"

It nodded, or at least she saw the top of its head bob behind the wings. "Yes 'Otto,' like the Germanic name, and 'el' meaning 'of God.'"

"Um, Ottoel, if you're an angel, shouldn't you be impervious to earthly weapons?"

"It still hurts."

"Oh, Jesus Christ—"

Under his breath, the angel quickly said, "In his name, amen."

"Let me go get you a washcloth."

She went to the bathroom and grabbed a washcloth, getting it good and sopping wet. She returned and handed it to Ottoel.

"Thank you," he said, scrubbing the area around his eyes vigorously. After several minutes, he pulled the washcloth from his face. "Ow. Ow. Ow. The water somehow makes it worse." He looked around frantically. "I need fresh air." He rushed over and stuck his head out the window. A few minutes later, he returned, his eyes puffy and red.

Amy held in a chuckle. He looked more like a demon than an angel now. Still, she had seen the wings. "So, um, Ottoel. What brings you here, in the middle of the night?"

Ottoel sighed. "It's just when I happened to arrive on Earth. I should have known to wait until morning, but I was really excited to meet you, America Mustang Love."

Amy held up her hand. "Please, just Amy is fine. But why are you here to see me?"

"Very well, Amy. I am here to ask for your assistance in a matter of great importance."

Amy felt her brow furrow. "Why?"

"Why what?"

"Why would you, an angel, ask for my help?"

Ottoel looked somewhat confused and then answered, "Because you are a holy warrior." He squeezed his eyes shut for a few seconds, and then opened them wide.

"Excuse me? I'm a what?"

"When you were born, your father asked for a miracle. You were not slated to survive, but he promised God that he would raise you to be a holy warrior and fight for the glory of God."

"My father, the lawyer, promised to raise me as a 'holy warrior?' Are you crazy?"

"Not at all." He seemed reasonably sure of himself.

"So, it was like a deal with the devil, except it was a deal with God, as in The One True?"

Ottoel nodded. "That's pretty much it."

If someone had asked Amy yesterday whether she believed in good and evil, God and the Devil, she'd have laughed in their face. Still, she had met two creatures of absolute evil, her stepmother and David Graves. And either she was talking to an angel, or some humanoid creature with wings, maybe some kind of alien bird man... Or maybe one of the cops had slipped her some acid. She didn't feel like she was hallucinating, though. Wouldn't she be staring at the back of her hand or having an out-of-body experience, not macing angels?

She still felt like she was experiencing a bit of shock, and she hadn't quite grasped the reality of a supernatural creature sitting in her apartment. She felt like she should ask the angel something of great import, but the only thing that occurred to her was quite trivial.

"Wait a minute, an angel arriving in the middle of the night with a booming voice—You're ripping off that movie *Karma*."

Ottoel shook his head. "No, I'm not. Besides, the middle of the night seemed practical—no interruptions, no danger of being seen. I've never even seen any Jason Sizemore movies."

"How did you know it was a Jason Sizemore movie?"

"I'm an angel. I know lots of things." He sounded kind of defensive.

"So, the angel showed his featureless crotch in that movie. Are you going to do that now?"

Ottoel looked a little offended by this question. "Please, Amy. My genitals are my business." He paused for a moment. "And failing to think of a better segue, maybe we should get down to business."

"About how I'm a holy warrior and you need my help. Doesn't the Vatican have some kind of paramilitary force, like an all-priest karate team?"

"Well, there is the *Capax Dei*. They're kind of like the anti-demon militia."

"Sounds good. Call them in. Because you've made a mistake. I'm not holy or a warrior. Now, if you needed a hand in a drinking contest, I might be able to help."

"And yet you defeated me, an angel, after being taken by surprise."

Amy bit her lip. "It's just pepper spray. I bought it at the gas station. I was almost molested by a frat boy the other night. Don't you think this holy warrior stuff would have kicked in then?"

Ottoel shrugged. "Search me. I'm just an angel, not the Almighty."

Amy rolled her eyes. "Sure, you don't know anything. And what kind of name is Ottoel anyway? I don't remember there being any Ottoel in the Bible."

"Oh yes," he said in a sarcastic tone. "Millions of angels out there, but you get all excited by the ones named in the book."

"Okay. I see your point."

"You know, there's only three in the Bible: Gabriel, Michael and Raphael, and trust me, if any one of them shows up, the shit has really hit the fan." He paused. "Do you still say that down here? I've been away for about thirty years, so my idioms might be out of date."

Amy nodded. "Yeah. People say that."

"Word. But we're getting off track again. I'm here to command you..." He paused dramatically, which Amy thought was a little too hammy. "...to take the job with Tommy Norman."

"What? No."

"You can't say no. The Lord commands you."

"Well, let me think about it, at least."

"Very well, Amy. Until then, I'm going to grant you a boon."

"A *what's-it?*"

He walked forward, and despite the fact she pulled back a little on him, he reached out and touched her shoulder. She felt her right side tingle.

"What the hell was that?"

"Just a little liver cleanse. Healing is one of my abilities, and quite frankly, I've read your file. You needed it."

"I have a file? Like a permanent record? Like in high school?"

Ottoel nodded. "Everyone has a file. We can read every detail of your life. Every thought. Every action."

Amy made a face. "Jesus."

"In his name, amen."

She thought of a few things she did in college and blushed. "Did you read the whole thing?"

He shrugged. "Just the past couple years. Don't worry about it. Humanity is messy and complicated." He looked up. "And I'm not the one who will judge you."

They shared a moment of uncomfortable silence.

"Anywho," Ottoel said, "I think I should be going."

"Are you going to disappear in a puff of smoke?"

"I thought I'd use the door." He walked to the apartment door and showed himself out. Amy noticed he'd kept the washcloth. Fair enough.

○ ○ ○

Amy did give going to work for Tommy Norman serious thought. The family members she didn't necessarily like and the god she hadn't really believed in both seemed to think it was a good idea. And while she didn't like taking advice from anyone, let alone her stepfamily, she'd never been given advice by a deity before.

The next morning, she waited until 8 AM, early enough to contact a relative about something important, and called her father.

He picked up on the third ring. "America, sweetie. Is everything all right? You aren't calling me to tell me about a new job, are you?" She'd always thought he sounded a little bit like the cartoon character, Yosemite Sam. She was reasonably sure he'd cultivated the accent to sound folksier in front of a jury.

"Well, Debbie set up an interview for me, but I'm not sure I'm going to take it."

"But why—"

"Dad! Listen for a minute. I need to ask you something extremely important."

"Of, course, darling. You know you can ask me anything.

"Did you possibly, just maybe, give away my life in servitude to Jesus, or something?"

He paused. "You were a very sick little girl. I *may* have said something to that effect. But people do those things all the time. They bargain with God. They offer impossible things in return for favors."

"Well, good news," she said sarcastically. "Because they were listening. Last night I was visited by an angel who told me I had to become a 'holy warrior,' whatever the fuck that means."

"Watch your language, young lady. Seriously, honey. I just said some typical prayers while you were lying in an incubator. Everyone does that kind of stuff. I was at a low point, and I'd just lost your mother." He paused. "Speaking of which, how are things going for you? You said you saw an angel. Is that some kind of metaphor?"

Amy took in a deep breath and slowly let it out. Her father clearly knew something, but was also living in some weird state of denial. It obviously bothered him, and she didn't want to pick at any old scabs involving her mother's death, so she lied. "It's okay, Dad. I just had a bad dream last night, and I woke up disoriented. It happens."

"Okay, but if you get too stressed out and need to relax, remember you always have a home here."

"Of course, Dad."

She hung up the phone and thought about making a resume. Didn't Holden have a computer? Maybe it was time for a bribe.

An hour later, she stood outside Holden's door with fast-food breakfast sandwiches. He answered the door in a bathrobe, his hair sticking up in the air. "Amy, what's up?"

"A bribe." She held up the greasy bag of goodness. "Breakfast. I need to use your computer."

Holden looked at the bag and immediately started to look a little green. "Why do you need a computer?"

"I'm applying for a job with Tommy Norman. I need to write a cover letter and resumé."

"The tech guy? Isn't he a war criminal?"

"Probably."

He started to laugh, then seemed to think better of it. "You think your current job is too demanding, but you're going to work for a guy who tried to start a civil war?"

"It's a family thing, don't ask. And apparently, he is no longer wanted for insurrection in Bolivia."

He looked ready to argue the point further, but then he seemed to turn a deeper shade of green. He got a faraway look in his eyes. "I'm sorry. I'm still feeling the effects of last night's Bacchanalia. Why are you so perky?"

"I've been doing a liver cleanse. Bacchanalia? Who talks like that, Holden?"

He tried to answer, but then his hand clamped over his mouth.

"Okay, why don't you go throw up, and I'll start writing my resumé?"

He turned and fled to the bathroom, from which came the sounds of ultimate suffering.

The sound of Holden retching made it hard to concentrate, and she didn't really want the job anyway—even with a kind of divine directive—so she looked at the sample resumé she'd downloaded, shrugged, and changed the name to hers. Done.

○ ○ ○

Two days later, Amy sat in the lobby of the Des Moines offices of Norman, LLC, wearing her best interview outfit. She was uncomfortable, partly because she was about to interview for a job she knew nothing about based on the strength of a fake resumé she hadn't read, partly because a super-glued bra had been digging into her side. She needed to follow through with her plan and replace them.

The lobby was well-appointed. The walls were freshly painted, with high, hardwood wainscot, and decorated with photos of Norman on magazine covers and expensive-looking art, not the sad stuff you found in most waiting rooms and hotel lobbies. Even the clock on the wall was a work of art, a huge hammered-bronze sculpture of the Sun with a tiny clock face in the middle. The carpet was thick. The chairs were soft leather. The receptionist desk rose regally above it all like the bench of a federal judge. But the desk itself was empty.

The room was so silent she could hear the clock ticking. Every tick resonated through the sculpture's bronze body, so instead of *click, click, click*, it went *ting, ting, ting*. Amy watched the minute hand close in on the top of the hour. Her interview was scheduled for 10:00 AM. It was 9:59.

She stood up and walked towards the large, oak panel door to the side of the receptionist's desk and turned the knob. It opened easily, and she walked down a hallway of offices. The offices were empty, and the nameplates by the doors were blank. She reached a T junction at the end of the hall. There was an emergency exit to the left, bathrooms to the right, and in front of her was an office with "T. Norman, CEO" on the nameplate.

She knocked.

The door opened, and before her stood Tommy Norman. Even with his name on the door, she wasn't prepared to meet the man himself. She had seen him in YouTube videos and photos from news reports while trying to learn what the company actually did, but she hadn't expected to see the big boss. She was surprised to see him in a suit rather than his usual look of shirtless and holding a rifle. Of course, that look didn't intimidate her, as it was also the Facebook profile picture of half the guys she'd gone to high school with. And she had to admit for an older dude, he was in pretty good shape, if you could get past the gray chest hair and his general greasiness.

He smiled at her. "Oh hi, Ms. Love. I'm sorry to keep you waiting. My receptionist is out today, and I'm on a call. Please wait in the lobby, and I'll be with you shortly." His accent was just as strange as people made it out to be—slow, slurred, and possibly eastern European. He'd already closed the door before she found time to respond.

So, she waited a few minutes more in the deserted lobby listening to the *ting, ting ting*. No one knew where Norman had gotten his accent. It was fairly well documented that he was born in Louisiana, where his father had been stationed. If questioned about the strangeness of the accent, he just said that his father was in the Army, and they traveled a lot.

At thirty minutes past the time her interview was meant to start, Amy was relatively sure Norman had forgotten about her. She might have been a little less concerned if there had been another human being to witness her abandonment.

Eventually though, Norman came through the lobby door. "Hi, Ms. Love." Or at least that's what she thought he was saying through his odd accent. From his inflection, he seemed surprised she had waited.

She was a little put off by his appearance. While he was wearing a suit, now she noticed that it was around three sizes too large for him. With his millions, you'd think he could afford a tailor. Maybe he just didn't have time for clothes that fit.

He said something to her as they were walking to the office, but he was harder to understand with his back turned. She answered him with a non-committal, "Hmmm."

"Have a seat, Ms. Love."

"Please, call me Amy." She sat down, smoothing her skirt.

"So..." He paused for a moment.

She mentally prepared herself for one of the standard interview questions, like where she wanted to be in five years.

"What do you think about multi-verse theory?"

"Well, um..." She had not been ready for that question. However, she did have an answer. "I find the theory interesting, although I'm not sure we'll ever be able to develop an experiment which can reach through to another universe and prove it correct."

After that, he followed up with more typical interview questions, but near the end of the interview, he asked, "What do you think of the belief some people hold that the world ended in 2012, and that we were transported to a new Earth which is a tiny bit different than the original?"

"I'm not so sure I buy that one," she said. "But if it did, it didn't affect my life at all."

"Very skeptical of you. I like someone who doesn't just blindly accept ideas. What is your position on God and the Devil?"

"Um, until recently, I've been pretty ambivalent, but lately I've seen some stuff that's bringing me around to the idea of the supernatural."

"Quantum Physics?"

She shrugged. "A little outside my area of expertise."

"And the Butterfly Effect."

"I haven't seen it, but I'm a big Ashton Kutcher fan in general. He's an Iowan, you know."

He nodded. "Now, would you stand on one leg and cluck like a chicken for me?"

"Excuse me?"

He flapped his arms in demonstration and said, "Chick, chick, chick, chick." Amy was pretty sure that wasn't how humans imitated chickens clucking.

She didn't move. "That doesn't sound like the kind of thing I would do. Does the job depend on it? I suppose I could learn."

He shook his head. "No, don't worry about it. I just wondered what you would do for job." Again, the way he said, *do for job*, made him sound like he was not a native English speaker. "So, are there any questions you would like to ask?"

Actually, there was something bothering Amy. She'd seen it while they were talking, and she had to ask about it. She pointed to one of the photos on the wall. "Is that you with Saddam Hussein?"

He shrugged. "That's just some guy I did consulting for back in the eighties. I don't like to talk the past. I prefer to look towards to the future."

Amy had no idea what to say to this. He clearly wanted people to know about his past. Not only did he have this picture, but a whole section of the lobby was a brag wall celebrating Tommy Norman.

He switched tone suddenly. "Would you like to start tomorrow?"

"Start what?" she asked. His question had been sudden, and she was still struggling a bit to parse his accent. She'd been caught off-guard.

"Working for me. You can begin tomorrow if you'd like." He handed her a business card. "Here's my personal number if you have any questions."

Despite having no time to think it through and not really understanding what she would be doing, she found herself nodding. Something about the man's charisma had drawn her in, like a used car salesman she knew she couldn't trust but wanted to anyway. She didn't know if she'd stay forever, but she did believe she wanted to stay long enough to find out more about the enigma that was Tommy Norman.

○ ○ ○

The next couple days were about what Amy expected from working an office job. She filled out forms and sent them back to Norman LLC's main US office in California. She played on the computer waiting for someone to give her something to do. She met the receptionist, a woman in her forties named Roselin who dressed about twenty years too young. Amy was pretty sure, both by her dress and some comments she had dropped during their short time working together, that Roselin was a regular at every local bar's "Cougar Night." Not Amy's choice of lifestyle, but to each their own.

When she went home on her third day, she still hadn't been given a task. She was just about to change into casual clothes when she got a text from Tommy Norman. "Meet me in front of your building in fifteen minutes. Dress nice."

This surprised her. She hadn't really talked about job duties or hours with anyone yet. Was she going to get overtime? And her outfit. How nice was nice? Fifteen minutes wasn't a lot of time to change, but she'd worn a cute top and black slacks, nice enough unless his cryptic wording meant formal wear. She refreshed her makeup, tightened her power bun, and called it good enough.

She expected the great Tommy Norman to pull up in a super sports car or something like that. Instead, he pulled up in a black Ford Explorer. She opened the passenger door and got in. He was wearing a business suit as he usually did, but if she wasn't misjudging, this one almost fit.

"Oh hi, Amy!" He somehow seemed surprised to see her even though he'd been the one to come get her.

"Hi, Mr. Norman. Nice car."

"Please, call me Tommy. I like the Explorer, quite economical, yes? Very good for the mountain roads in Bolivia."

"I was expecting you to drive some kind of super-car."

"No. Not me. All that power makes them hard to drive. They rarely have comfortable seats, and they never have cup holders. I don't go for flashy things like that."

Judging by the condition of his suits, she believed him.

"I didn't realize my duties would include going out in the evenings," Amy said, hoping to get more information about the actual nature of her job.

"Oh, don't worry about it. There's just a lot going on right now. Once things settle down, this won't be a regular thing. But tonight, I'll take you to a nice restaurant, maybe have some nice food. A nice time."

"Sure. Sounds... um... nice." Actually, it sounded like a date. She hoped he didn't expect that kind of a relationship from his employees.

They drove the rest of the way in silence. And Tommy parked the car in front of *Rosa*, a high-end Italian restaurant. "Have you ever been here before?" Tommy asked.

"No, but I've heard good things."

She followed Tommy to the front door, pleased he hadn't tried to grab her arm and "escort" her. When they reached the maitre d', he said, "Tommy Norman. I'm in the David Graves party."

Amy felt her heart start to beat hard. They were here to see David Graves—embodiment of all evil, fired her from Calltelestar, David Graves? As she followed a server through the dining room, her legs trembled, threatening to give out. They didn't stop in the dining room either. They went through the kitchen, to a back, private room.

Around a table sat three people, her stepsister, a gray-haired man, and a weaselly-looking man with slicked-back hair. She relaxed for a moment until she heard *his* voice from the corner of the room. "Welcome, Mr. Norman."

Tommy smiled his greasy smile. "Oh, hi, David. Hi, Debbie. Hi, Dick Storm. Hi, Dick Storm's friend."

Graves was standing behind a bar that took up an entire wall of the room. To either side of him stood a bartender. He paused. "America Love? Nice to see you again. It looks like you've fallen up." He popped the top off a bottle of Champagne. "Who wants a glass of Dom?"

The gray-haired man shook his head. "Perhaps later. Perhaps you could find me an espresso?"

"Same for me," said his greasy-haired companion.

He turned to Debbie. "Mineral water,' she said.

Graves smiled, pouring himself a glass. "I'm sure we could do that. Mr. Norman?"

"You better call me Tommy, eh? Do you have any carrot juice?"

"A carrot juice it is, and Amy?"

"Um, actually I'd like to try the Dom." She knew she wasn't going to like it, but it was open, and at a few hundred dollars a bottle, she had to try it.

Graves carried over two Champagne flutes. He set one in front of Amy and kept the other for himself. The two bartenders came back with mineral water and espresso, and Amy was surprised that they managed carrot juice for Mr. Norman.

Tommy raised his glass, took a drink and winced. "It doesn't taste too good, but my body is temple."

All Amy could think was that Tommy's "temple" was a little on the greasy side and needed a better tailor. Also, wasn't he famous for cocaine use? She smiled at him and sipped her Champagne. As she expected, she didn't actually like it; it was too dry for her taste. Unlike, Tommy, however, her body was not a temple, and if she had to sit at a meeting with David Graves, she wasn't going to do it sober. She took another, not so small, sip.

"At the risk of being gauche, gentlemen," Debbie said, "perhaps we should get down to business. We have two companies, Calltelestar Peopleconnect, represented by Mr. David Graves, and MediaStorm LLC. represented by Mr. Dick Storm. We've done the preliminary work, and we have all but the paperwork done on the financial disclosures. Are we going to merge these companies together?" She started talking about federal laws and approval. Amy took the opportunity to grab the bottle and pour another glass of Dom.

Dick Storm spoke first. "I want fifty-five percent."

Graves chuckled. "Dick, if you're going to be like that, I might as well walk. Calltelestar isn't worth as much as MediaStorm on paper, but we're bringing the technology you want to the table. You really didn't think we'd give you controlling interest, did you?"

Storm looked annoyed. "Please! Don't give me fairy tales about unrealized potential. MediaStorm has one million subscribers, almost no competition, and a lot more liquidity. That's what we're bringing to the table, not a list of phone numbers of people who don't want to hear from you. We're talking about a million people using our service every day, paying us anything we want, begging us for help when their precious service goes out, influencing what they see on TV and what websites they go to. You annoy the people you call. We control our customers."

"As long as we're making demands, gentlemen," Tommy said. "I expect fifteen percent for my contribution."

"That's outrageous," Graves said. "You want me to give you my dick too?"

Norman smiled. "If you want to roll out Calltelestar's proprietary software over MediaStorm's network, you need my help. Without me, you have no merger. You can't just walk over to IBM or Microsoft for a job like this. You need me. And trust me, David. I have plenty in the trouser department. No need to put your dick on the table."

Amy, well into her second glass of Dom, was feeling quite loopy. Alcohol didn't usually affect her so strongly. She was having trouble following the conversation, but there seemed to be a lot of talk about dicks. She slapped the table, and there was blessed silence. "Can we stop measuring dicks? I thought we were here to talk about a merger." Actually, she'd just learned about this a few minutes ago, but she'd slapped the table, and she figured she better follow up with something. Why was she so drunk? She gulped down a bit more of the Dom.

Debbie interjected. "Amy makes a good point. If this goes well, there will be more than enough to go around, the money included."

Graves smiled the cute little smile he'd used when he was firing Amy. "Our technology isn't a fairy tale, Dick. I know how much you want it. You aren't going to walk out of here with the majority share. We don't need your subscribers that badly."

Dick Storm glowered at everyone, but then he said, "How about I take forty percent. Calltelestar can take fifty percent, and Norman can have ten?"

Norman pointed at Graves, Storm, and himself. "Forty-nine, thirty-nine, twelve. In the event of a disagreement, I want to be the tie-breaker."

Storm nodded. "Fine by me, but I want you to fire all my customer support people. They're annoying."

Graves nodded. "This seems like a reasonable offer. I have to take this back to my president and the board. You two only answer to yourself. I'll go back to them and pitch this."

The guy with the slicked back hair next to Dick Storm spoke for the first time. "No. I don't think that's good enough. You came to this meeting to make a deal, so make the deal." He stood up and pounded on the table, which woke up Amy, who was feeling very drunk and relaxed. She poured herself another glass of Dom; it was growing on her.

Graves stood up, and the two men were almost nose to nose. "If you demand an immediate answer about giving up control of our company, it's a hard no. This meeting is meant to be a negotiation in good faith. I'm not going to be bullied into a rushed deal."

The slicked-back hair guy shook his head. "Oh, Graves. You still don't have a set of balls, do you?"

Amy shook her head in amazement. "Why are we talking about male sex organs again?"

The slicked-back hair guy turned to gawk at Amy. "Don't you know who this is? He's the lapdog of the two guys who really run Calltelestar. He's the guy who fires people for having sex with the coffee machine and stupid shit like that."

Graves nodded, and his voice took on a tone of realization. "Hey, I remember you. You were the number two guy in Circle Three. I canned you a few years ago... Eric Driscoll, right?"

"So, you do remember me, asshole. Calltelestar hired me away from a good job, lured me across the country to fucking Des Moines. Then you fire me and contest my unemployment. Told every person who called the company that I'd sexually assaulted my supervisor's teenage daughter. My supervisor was Randy Clarke; he doesn't even have a daughter. My fiancé left me because of you. You utter bastard." He'd gotten extremely red in the face, and with his last three words, he'd poked Graves hard in the chest. "I've wanted a piece of you for years—"

With no hint of emotion or even being upset, Graves kneed the guy in the groin and punched him in the face when he bent over. Amy had never seen anyone actually fly backward from a punch, like they did in movies. It was impressive and scary, and the idea of Graves beating someone up in a business meeting seemed so absurd, Amy found herself giggling. She looked over to Tommy Norman and found her boss had pulled a pistol from inside his jacket. He held it casually, as if he was used to that sort of thing.

Storm stood up and walked over to his downed man. Picking him up off the floor, he said, "Get with your people, Graves. I'll overlook this kind of thing once, but I'm a businessman. I don't want any more of this old-school shit."

Graves looked amused. "Old school? He came at me, and I didn't even stab him." He somehow produced a foot long dagger from under his suit jacket. It was formidable, with jewels and demons carved on it. A little gauche for Amy's taste, but definitely something Crocodile Dundee would acknowledge as a knife. "And trust me. I came prepared."

This earned another glare from Storm. When Storm had dragged his man out of the room, Graves sat back down. "I think that went well."

Tommy slipped the gun back inside his jacket without comment.

Amy pointed at his dagger. "I think pulling that out still qualifies as dick stuff."

This made Tommy laugh out loud. He even sprayed a bit of carrot juice.

"Amy," Debbie said, "I'm going to go to the bathroom. Come with me."

"What?"

"Bathroom. Now."

Amy nodded. She thought she better tell her boss. "I have to go to the bathroom."

Norman shrugged. "Okay with me." He set down his carrot juice. "I think that's healthy enough for today. Graves, how about a Scotch?"

Debbie pulled Amy to her feet and half-dragged her to the ladies' room. "You're drunk."

"Yes, I am," Amy agreed. "But I shouldn't be. I've only had three glasses of Dom Perin-nom-nom-nom. Or is it four? I've lost count."

She dropped Amy onto the sink. "Be sick if you have to."

"No, my stomach is fine." Her attempt to assess her stomach made her think of something else. This was the first time she'd had a drink since Ottoel had visited her. "I know!"

"You know what?" Debbie turned on the cold tap.

"I have a new liver."

"That would be a miracle."

"Exactly."

Debbie pushed Amy closer to the sink and splashed cold water on her face. "Does that help?"

"My face is wet," Amy complained, "I'm cold, and you messed up my makeup." She grabbed some paper towels from the dispenser and tried to scrub off the worst of the damage, it left her skin looking red and irritated, but did nothing to actually help.

Debbie yanked her out of the sink and slapped her, not hard—she knew what Debbie's slaps were like when she meant them. This was just a little pick-me-up. "You're embarrassing me. Now you're going to go out there and keep your mouth shut."

They walked back to the table, and Amy plunked down next to Tommy Norman.

Tommy nodded to her. "I think the negotiations are over for the night. I can take you home, unless you want me to buy dinner. I mean, we are here, and we do have to eat."

Amy made a face. "I'm not really in the mood." Actually, she looked like hell, and she was feeling a little queasy.

He walked her to the parking lot, and once they were on their way, he asked, "What did you think of that negotiation?"

"It was a little easy, wasn't it?"

He smiled. "Easy, but not too easy. There's too much money on the table and everyone knew what to expect. I'm getting overpaid, but they know I'm the only one who can do the job, and this way neither of those two is guaranteed the upper hand. Nobody's going to walk away from a table with a quarter billion dollars on it. Besides, Calltelestar and MediaStorm are after more than just money. MediaStorm needs the technology, and Calltelestar needs the subscriber base."

"Um, Mr. Norman."

"Please, call me Tommy."

"Okay, Tommy. Why did you bring me in on this? I mean, I don't even own a computer, and I'm not a businessperson."

"Well, you did go to Columbia for business, didn't you?"

She was confused for a moment. Then she remembered the fake resumé she hadn't read. She wondered if he meant the college or the country. "Oh, I um... I... Well..." she stammered. She couldn't think of anything to say.

Tommy laughed out loud. "Don't worry about it. I know that wasn't your resumé. Your sister gave me your background. You worked for your father, managing his office before you could drive a car. You trained as a paralegal, but you dropped out because you were bored. I dropped out of MIT for the same reason."

Amy had watched a documentary about Tommy Norman, and she knew for a fact that he'd been kicked out of the graduate program at MIT for sleeping with an undergrad he was supposed to be teaching.

"I need someone to watch over my Des Moines office when I can't be around, which hopefully will be most of the time, because every day I spend in Des Moines is a day I'm not on the beach surrounded by pretty girls in bikinis. That means going to meetings with me so you're in the loop, and also going to meetings for me when I can't be here. It also means being the local business manager and buying office supplies so I don't have to. Just consider yourself half regional manager, half intern."

"Wonderful," Amy said, hoping that he would spend as little time in Iowa as possible. There was nothing greater than working for an elderly man who saw women as props in his own personal fantasy. "Wait a minute, what beach? I thought Bolivia was land locked."

"I have a lake house."

She nodded. "Ah." She closed her eyes, and she must have fallen asleep. She awoke with a start when Norman said, "Amy, you're home." She looked through the window and saw her apartment building.

"Okay. Thanks for the ride."

She went upstairs and collapsed on her bed, which spun under her. "Ottoel, I'm going to kick your butt."

He appeared beside her. "What for?"

She jumped. "Holy shit! Where did you come from?"

"I heard your prayer. You called on me. You wish to kick me in the rear end?" He seemed confused by this.

"Okay, explain to me, one thing." She paused thinking these words were in the wrong order somehow. "Fuck, still drunk, I am." She paused to parse what she'd just said. "Talking like Yoda, I am."

"You're intoxicated again. Let me help." Ottoel did something, and Amy suddenly felt sober, like she'd been plunged into a cold lake.

"Wow, that's impressive." She stopped to evaluate if her words were coming out in the right order.

"Just a minor miracle. I turned the alcohol in your system to water. Wine into water, if you will." He smiled at his own joke.

Amy didn't find it funny, but something did occur to her. "You can work miracles? Can you fix bras?"

"What?" Ottoel looked confused.

"Never mind. I'll explain later. Why didn't you tell me David Graves was involved in this deal?"

"I was not specifically instructed to. Was that detail important to you?"

"Yes. You know he's totally evil, don't you?"

Ottoel shrugged. "You may be surprised by how much goodness he has left in him. I'm just following my orders. You might want to ask your employer about the purpose of the merger."

"I assume they're expecting to make a boat-load of money."

"Among other things."

Amy watched him for some kind of clue about what he was talking about, but he was silent. "I'm still mad at you, you know. I thought you were going to give me a super liver. You gave me the liver of a child."

"Technically, no. For the lack of a better term, I reset your body to factory settings. Just go easy on it for a few weeks, and you'll be healthier than ever. It just needs some breaking-in time."

"A few weeks. Now you tell me. I just got drunk off my ass in front of my boss. Okay, well, I intended to get drunk, but I was wasted."

"Oh dear. That's no good. Now, just abstain from alcohol or any hard drugs for the next four weeks or so. I performed a genuine miracle. That's not a trivial thing."

Amy sighed. "Right, four weeks. No fun. I might as well go back to Holstein." Even as she said it, she knew there was no way she'd actually do it.

5

Lawyers, Guns, and Manicures

David Graves walked through the front door of his beautiful, modern home, and his girlfriend slapped him across the back of the head.

"Ow! What was that for?"

Raven wore a black nightie that made her look like a sexy angel of death. Then again, no matter what she wore, she looked like a sexy angel of death. Her current attire just accentuated that appearance.

To tell the truth, she looked at home with the decor of their foyer and living room, full of matte black furniture, floored in black marble tile, accented with dark earth tones. Matt Rose, David's former boss, had done the decorating himself. He'd also designed the ritual room underneath Calltelestar. David wasn't sure if he just liked black marble everything or he stole the materials from work.

"That's for staying out half the night. Where have you been?"

"I had a business meeting. Then I had dinner at *Rosa.*"

"Were you with that Debbie woman?"

"She's an attorney. Your father hired her. Besides, she's not my type. You know I'm only interested in you."

Accepting his compliment, she changed the subject. "The police have been digging up the neighbor's yard all day. Did you have anything to do with that?"

David shrugged, and Raven slapped him again.

"I was supposed to go to the fucking spa in Jordan Creek with Ruth in three days. Now her husband's in jail, so I'm not going to get my spa day."

"I'm sorry. I had to do something. His parties were driving me nuts. I'm sick of waking up to karaoke versions of *Dancing Queen* in the middle of the night. I thought this was a good, subtle solution. I'm just trying to be a good Satanist. Isn't that what we're supposed to do, inflict harm on our enemies in as swift and cruel a fashion as possible? I even hit a guy at the meeting tonight. Totally gratuitous."

"I don't care who you hit or fuck over. But for the love of Satan, it better not interrupt my spa day." She briefly examined her nails and made a face. "These gel nails look like crap if you let them go too long."

When Dave first met Raven, she always had cracked nails with oil under them. Now she went to spa days with Ruth and got manicures. While he didn't care for the change, he knew enough not to tell Raven how to live her life or groom herself as he valued his genitals and wished to keep them attached.

"I'm going to bed," Raven announced. "If you know what's good for you, don't follow me."

David sighed as she turned her back and walked away. He remembered when she used to threaten him for not coming to bed, but like many relationships, theirs was complicated. He had been tricked into selling his soul, and he tried to be the best bad guy he could be. She was a half demon with anger management issues. Still, she was threatening him. With Raven, he'd be more worried if the threats ever stopped.

He walked over to the black marble bar and poured himself a Scotch. The Scotch, like pretty much everything else in the house, reminded him of Matt Rose, the man he murdered and whose life he now lived. He'd received Rose's belongings when he murdered him. It was some kind of old Satanist tradition. So, he lived in Rose's house. He ate at *Rosa,* Rose's restaurant.

And he drank Rose's Scotch—he'd found thirty cases of the stuff in the basement, behind Rose's sex dungeon. Every bottle worth over a hundred dollars, some much more. He figured he should either take up the habit or auction it off. It seemed easier to drink it. He poured a tall glass of *Glen something or other* and walked out to the back porch, which gave him a perfect view to watch the police dig up Donnie and Ruth's rose garden.

About halfway through his glass of Scotch, he began to get nostalgic. He used to be an innocent, good person. He didn't drink expensive Scotch, own a big house, or drive a Lexus, but he was happy. Well, to be honest with himself, he wasn't really happy back then, but he certainly wasn't happy now.

He kind of felt the same about Raven. They used to fight all the time, but they also used to make up, usually through athletic sex. Now, she went to bed early, and he fell asleep drunk on the black leather couch. They had turned into the world's most boring evil power couple.

He was beginning to drift off when the backhoe operator yelled for the policemen. They had found a body in the rose garden.

For a moment, David wondered if Raven had murdered someone and hidden them in the neighbor's garden. While he was relatively sure she didn't kill people in her spare time, it was in her DNA. Then he began to wonder if Donnie actually *was* a mass murderer. It made sense in a way. Who, other than a psychopath, would sing ABBA at high volume in a residential neighborhood at one in the morning?

○ ○ ○

Late that night, in the depths of the MediaStorm offices, Dick Storm put on his black robe. He sat in the middle of the pentagram in his meditation room and lit a single black candle. The negotiation had not gone as well as he had hoped. Eric had made a fool of himself, as usual. Still, they would get a fair share of the new company.

He tried to clear his mind and reach out to the fiber optic cables surrounding him. He could feel people's fears, lusts, and desires pouring through those cables. He tried to pull a sip of that power into his body, but it was difficult. His mind was unfocused.

When he'd hired Eric, he intended to make him his successor. A disbarred lawyer with a history of debt collection who'd happily sold his soul because, in his words, he wasn't using it, seemed like the perfect person to run MediaStorm while Dick retired in comfort and waited to take his place in Hell. But in the end, he had to face facts. As much as he liked Eric, the man was too short sighted to run a company like MediaStorm. He could never see the big picture, which was probably why Calltelestar had fired him.

Perhaps this Calltelestar merger was exactly the thing he needed. He could retire, leaving Eric as a vice president in the merged company with no hard decisions to make, a simple job that would take care of Eric for life. This was another good reason not to push too hard for a controlling interest in the new company. It wasn't like he would let Eric run things. Besides, they had a good team over there. Graves was the golden boy, but the rest of the team was top notch as well, every one of them a powerful Satanic wizard. Meanwhile, he was having trouble pulling in the powerful emotions of his cable subscribers. Maybe it was time to up their energy levels, maybe offer a free week of Cinemax. He couldn't wait to see what they could do with Calltelestar's soul-sucking technology.

He unfolded himself from his trance-pose, took off his cloak, hung it up, and sighed. Lately, he'd been a little bored with it all. He'd dedicated his life to making money and serving Satan, and now that he was a little older, he no longer desired all the pleasures of flesh those things could give him. He'd gone to orgies with Hollywood celebrities, but now all he really wanted was to cuddle up with a good book and someone he really cared about. He should have asked for eternal youth along with the package.

He took the back way out of the MediaStorm building to avoid any employees that may have been working late, along with the overnight customer support people, who weren't great conversationalists. They were all obsessed with some video game, Fortnite. At least it kept them from helping the customers.

When he slipped out the back door, a man stood by his Jaguar. As he approached, the man said, "Are you Storm?"

"What would make you think that?"

"You're the only one with a hundred-thousand-dollar car in the lot."

"Well, you're wrong. I'm Mike Dexter, Mr. Storm's accountant."

The guy glared at Storm and held up his phone, where a Des Moines Register article showed Storm under the title, "Worst Customer Service in Nation."

Storm shrugged. "Why did you bother to ask if you already knew who I was?"

The man seemed to ponder this for a moment before pressing on, refusing to be derailed. "I haven't had Internet for four weeks. I lost my job because of it. And your company just sent me a bill for two hundred dollars. I know it's wrong. I can't go over my data caps because I don't have service."

"You can take it up with customer service—"

"You don't think I've called? Every day? For the last three weeks? The only advice I got was to try out some game—"

Storm nodded. "Fortnite."

"Which I can't play because I don't have Internet. I just lost the best job I ever had. I got to work from home, in my robe and slippers. That was my dream job, Storm. You ruined my dream."

As the man's voice rose in pitch and tears streamed from his eyes, Storm checked his watch. This wasn't the first time someone had confronted him. It probably wouldn't be the last.

Then, the disgruntled customer did something unusual. He reached into his jacket and pulled out a gun.

"Are you a Star Wars fan?" Storm asked.

"What?" This put the man off his game. Now instead of angry, he was confused.

"You know, Luke Skywalker, Wookies, Yoda, and shit."

"Um, yeah. I guess so."

"Oh good. Then you'll like this trick." Storm went through a little mantra in his head and called on one of the powers that had been gifted to him by the Dark Lord. Lightning shot out from his fingers and burned deep into the man, who screamed and fell to the ground.

Storm grabbed hold of the man's shirtsleeve, dragged him to the dumpster and threw him in. He said a little spell over the body that would disguise the corpse as garbage for a couple weeks. Then he retrieved the man's gun, a Smith and Wesson 9mm. A bit pedestrian, but hopefully it was licensed to the dead man who would never be found again. That could always come in handy.

As he walked back to the car, he found himself whistling a little tune. It felt good to murder someone once in a while. He didn't feel quite so bored anymore.

○ ○ ○

The next morning, Amy woke up feeling good. She found this confusing, as feeling good in the morning wasn't something she was familiar with. Maybe it had something to do with the miracle Ottoel had done to her. This reminded her, she really needed to ask him again about fixing her bras—it was either that or shop for new ones.

She got into the office early and immediately regretted it, as she really didn't have anything to do. Still, it was probably a good thing she had come in, because as soon as she sat down, Roselin the receptionist buzzed her phone.

Amy picked up the phone. "Yes?"

"There's a young lawyer here, a Mr. Labrador. He has some documents for the boss."

"Okay. I'll come get him."

"He's a cute one. I call dibs."

"Not a problem."

Amy double-checked that Tommy wasn't in his office, but he didn't seem to be around, so she walked to the lobby and opened the heavy, oak door. "Mr. Labrador?"

The only person in the lobby other than Roselin stood up. He wore a nice suit and had sandy-blond hair in a power cut. He walked toward her extending his hand to shake hers. "Hi. Call me Justice."

As she shook his hand and introduced herself, she took a close look at his face, expecting she'd want to be able to recognize him. But her gaze never rose over

87

his chin. It was the most cleft chin she had ever seen. She gazed into the abyss down the center, and she could see that he couldn't shave down inside the crevice, and little hairs lived inside. Some chins had little dimples. Justice Labrador's chin was the Grand Canyon.

"Please follow me, Mr. Labrador." She showed him through the door and started walking to her office. "Mr. Norman is out currently, but perhaps I can..." She turned around quickly. "Wait, you're the guy in the TV commercial with the midgets—the Iowa Law Dog."

He held up his hands. "Guilty, that's me. They actually prefer to be called little people." This seemed like a huge dose of political correctness from someone who dressed midg... little people up like police officers and whipped them for pulling over his drunk driving clients. "And you're Debbie's sister, Amy. I was told you have full authority to act as Mr. Norman's representative. Therefore, I am at your service."

She took him to her office and asked him to have a seat. "So tell me, why is my sister employing someone from another practice?"

He smiled a sheepish, cute, goofy smile that almost took her attention away from the chin. "To tell you the truth, I think she's doing me a favor. She's got summer associates and paralegals that can do this kind of work, but we were friends in law school. I think she threw me some business because this is a big deal and there's lots of money to go around. It's not easy having an independent practice. I still have to make enough to pay the rent."

"Very well, Mr. Labrador. What do you have for me?"

He handed her a large binder full of paper. "Pretty typical stuff, really. I've just summarized the independent audits of the two companies, filled out the boilerplate forms, and written in my recommendations. Debbie says they aren't really interested in the actual valuations; they're merging because Calltelestar has some sort of proprietary technology and Dick Storm wants to retire. Since both companies are privately-held, they can do pretty much whatever they want, but someone has to do the tedious paperwork to file with the government. Debbie says she asked me because I'm fast, and I don't make mistakes."

"And is that true, Mr. Labrador?"

"That I'm fast?" He winked at her. He actually winked at her. "That depends on what you mean by fast."

She decided to change the subject. "Privately held? I thought Calltelestar had all kinds of investors and a board of directors." Amy's law experience was more based in large family farms, which were often private corporations, but mostly for tax purposes.

Labrador nodded. "Yes, it does. But it doesn't issue stock that's traded on an exchange. That's the difference. If they were, their stockholders could sue them to stop the merger, not that they would, as on paper, it looks like Calltelestar is getting the better end of the deal. They might object to Tommy Norman taking a huge chunk of the company for what should be lower-priced work-for-hire. But again, it's their business. They can overpay if they want to."

"But why do they want to?" Honestly, Amy couldn't care less if Calltelestar, the company that fired her under false pretenses, and MediaStorm, which seemed to specialize in treating their customers like dirt, both disappeared into bankruptcy and obscurity, but apparently being involved in this merger was not only her job, but also part of God's plan, so she figured she better pay attention.

"I don't really understand it myself, but they think that Tommy Norman can bring something to their source code that other people can't." He gave her his really cute smile again. "Hey, I have to get going. I have to be in court in thirty minutes. Trust me, judges do not like it if you show up late. Why don't we continue this at dinner, around seven, at *Rosa*?"

At hearing the name of David Grave's restaurant, Amy shook her head violently. She immediately said, "Not *Rosa*." As soon as she'd said it, she realized she'd implied that she was open to dinner at a different venue.

"No Italian, eh? How about the *Jade Bowl*?"

"I guess." She couldn't help but think she just made a horrible mistake. She didn't want to date anyone, especially a lawyer. There were enough lawyers in her life already. Also, he had described himself as a friend of her stepsister, which was shudder worthy.

"Great. It's a date." Before she could argue, he stood up. "Sorry again, but I really do have to run." He showed himself out.

○ ○ ○

Andy Nelson, the senior partner in her firm, looked up as Debbie walked into the office. He looked unhappy today, which was not unusual. She'd only seen him happy three times, and on all three of those occasions, he'd been eating steak.

She smiled and said, "You wanted to see me, Andy?"

"Yes, come in. Close the door." Asking to close the door was never a good sign.

She closed the door, sat down, and waited. No need to fill the air with noise. He'd asked her there.

After a moment, he spoke. "So, how are things going with this merger?"

"Quite well, really. There's a little bit of friction between Dick Storm's assistant and David Graves, but nothing I can't handle," she lied. If the two attacked each other again, she planned to hide under the table.

"Good. I'm sure it goes without saying how important this merger is to this firm. We gave this to you to run with so you could show us you're ready for partner."

90

Debbie took a deep breath to steady her nerves, so she could keep her cool, professional facade. "I understand."

She knew she couldn't be a senior associate forever. Her name had to go on the door, or she needed to look for work elsewhere. Becoming a young partner at a small, prestigious firm was the first major milestone in a long string of goals to leave her semi-retired and wealthy by the time she was fifty. If the timing worked out right, she might even buy her stepfather's practice in Holstein.

Nelson picked up a piece of paper from his desk. "I understand you've farmed out some work to this Justice Labrador fellow. The guy with the silly commercials. Why did you feel that was necessary? Don't his criminal clientèle keep him busy?"

"I suppose we could have done it in-house. But we had some perfunctory paperwork. Since the client was paying, I figured why tie-up any of our internal resources? Despite his somewhat... um... flamboyant advertising, I went to school with Labrador. He's a good lawyer and very detail oriented. He also might be a good resource to have in our pocket when our clients need work we don't want to put our names on."

He nodded. "Fine. Fine. But I think it goes without saying, if things don't work out with this merger, advancement in this firm will not be in your future." Despite it going *without saying,* he'd said it anyway. Either this merger went through without a hitch, or she might as well find somewhere else to work.

Of course, it wasn't fair. It would take a miracle worker to hold the deal together. Dick Storm was old but mean. Graves was amicable enough, but his bosses had their own agendas, and Tommy Norman was a computer genius, but he was also a paranoid conman. Still, what in life was fair?

6

A Date with Justice

After Justice left, Amy wondered what she should do next. She looked over the papers he'd dropped off, or at least she tried to look over them. They were boring. Many of the actual pages included long strings of numbers. She double-checked a few random pages, and the math balanced out. There was, indeed, a lot of money to go around. She waited until around two and decided to take a long, late lunch.

She went back to Paddy's, hoping to run into Holden. She didn't see him, but when she walked in, she saw Howard, the guy with the sharp features who was investigating the attack on the governor, and Seth, the bald cop with the mustache who had been looking into women loitering in men's rooms, having lunch in uniform. Seth saw her walk in and waved her over. "Amy, right? Holden's friend."

"Yeah, I was hoping to see him here."

"He's going to be busy for a while," Howard said. "Last night, someone phoned in an anonymous tip, bodies buried in a rose garden in some fancy gated community. They've found two full corpses and a foot so far." Seth nudged him, and Howard said, "Oh, I'm sorry, Amy. I didn't mean to talk shop. I hope I didn't put you off your lunch."

She shook her head. "No, I'm good. I find it all fascinating." She was just glad they were discussing a crime in which she was not personally involved. One thing bothered Amy, though. "Should you really be discussing such a high-profile case in public?"

"Well," Howard said, "pretty much everyone in the department knows what's going on. Plus, this is a cop bar." He pointed across from them. "...that's the sheriff and two senior deputies." He pointed to the next nearest table. "DEA." Another table. "County Attorney's office. Sometimes a local reporter sneaks in, but we know the crime reporters by sight."

Amy nodded. "Okay. Good enough."

"How are you doing?" Seth said. "You said you were quitting your job?"

Amy knew her current choice of jobs wouldn't go over well with these two, but she decided not to be coy about it. "Oh, I've been working for Tommy Norman for about a week now. Debbie got me the job."

The two men looked surprised for a second. Then Howard said, "I don't suppose you remember what I said about the website, Task Um?"

"I may remember something about that."

"Well, it turns out that site is owned by Tommy Norman. It took us a while to untangle it, but he launched it when he was living in Bolivia. Apparently, he found the time to make the site despite all the cocaine he did, or maybe because of it."

Now it was Amy's turn to feel shocked. She felt a chill so severe, her arms broke out in goosebumps. She felt like she should say something, but all she managed was a simple, "Oh, that's interesting."

Seth nodded gravely. "If I were you, I'd maybe think about moving to another job. Even if what you're doing is totally legit, he's into some weird stuff. You don't want to end up a scapegoat in one of his schemes."

Amy thought about how to answer this. She'd moved from Task.um, where she had unknowingly worked for Tommy Norman, to directly working for Tommy Norman. Did he know she'd already worked for him under Task.um? Was fate, or God, or whatever somehow pushing them together? Was she somehow tricked by one of them, and if so, why?

For some reason, an angel had asked her to work for Tommy Norman. What sense did that make? The angel had only shown up twice, both times late at night. Maybe there was a simple explanation, like she had a brain tumor and hallucinated him when she got tired. When you lived in a world where people believed they were Napoleon Bonaparte, seeing an angel a couple of times didn't seem like that large a delusion.

A call came through on Howard's radio; someone had collapsed at Walmart. Abruptly, he stood up. "That's right next door. We better go lend a hand until the ambulance guys show up." He checked in on the radio.

Seth got up and followed him out. "See you around, Amy."

Her food arrived, and with nothing to do but eat, she sent a text to Holden. "Still digging up body parts?"

He replied. "How'd you know?"

"I have my sources. Just had lunch at Paddy's with Seth and Howard."

"Things quiet since last night. Interviewing neighbors. Didn't you work for David Graves?"

"Yeah."

"He lives next door. Drank a bottle of Scotch and watched us dig all night."

"Sounds like something he'd do. He's all class."

Amy sighed and pushed her food aside. She didn't mind talking about dead bodies while she ate, but the mention of David Graves had turned her stomach.

○ ○ ○

Amy went back to her office, and with nothing else to do, she sat down and studied. First, she read a few money magazine and legal articles about how mergers happened in the real world. Then she looked at Justice Labrador's financial summary again.

Justice was right. From her minimal understanding of mergers between public companies, the deal they had set down at Rosa would never fly. Whether Calltelestar had some propriety technology or not, the owners of the company with the highest net worth should be getting the most shares in the merged company.

She went home early to prepare for her date. After all, she would be eating with an attorney working on the merger. That counted as work, didn't it?

She lay on her bed, contemplating what she wanted to wear when Holden texted her. "Hey, you home?"

"Yeah, want to come over?"

"Sure. I'm too tired to sleep."

He showed up fifteen minutes later, still damp from the shower. "I've been up all night digging in some guy's yard. It really sucked. I was so tired, I knocked on your neighbor's door. I could have sworn you were in Apartment Five."

Amy considered this a good turn of events. If Holden also remembered her in the other apartment, it seemed less likely that she was experiencing some kind

96

of grand hallucination, and more likely there was actually supernatural fuckery about. Still, Amy didn't feel like addressing the apartment issue. Instead, she asked about his work. "So, you got to dig up bodies last night?"

He made a face. "It kind of sucked. 'Got to' kind of implies it was something I enjoyed doing, not standing in a hole with a shovel and a dead body."

"Didn't you have like a backhoe or something?"

He shrugged. "Sure, but they can't risk tearing apart a corpse with heavy equipment. The body and anything on it has to be treated as evidence. Eventually somebody had to get down in the hole, and guess who the rookie is?"

Amy felt a little sick. "That's really gross."

"Then, when they thought they'd gotten all the bodies, I had to quickly clean up and ask all the neighbors if they'd seen anything. On the bright side, I got mentioned on the local news."

"Yeah?"

"One of the local stations incorrectly identified me as the officer heading up the case—because I interviewed the neighbors. Kind of lame, really. So," Holden said changing the subject, "how did you end up having lunch with Howard and Seth?"

"They were eating at Paddy's, and I was searching for sustenance. We only exchanged a few words before they had to run to help someone passed out at Walmart."

"So, what are you up to now?"

"I'm getting dressed for a date. Want to help me choose an outfit?"

He put his hands on his hips. "You know, it's a cliché to think every gay wants to play with women's clothes and dress up his girl friends like he's playing with Barbies."

Amy could tell he was joking. "Accepting the fact that not every gay guy would want that, how about the one standing right there?" She pointed at him.

He nodded. "Despite my dislike of the stereotypes, you are my friend, so I will hold my nose and render assistance." He walked to a nearby rack of clothes and started flipping through them. "Now, what do you want to say with your outfit?" He flipped through a few and held up an illustrious little black dress. "I'm a *femme fatale?*" He put it away and pulled out a low-cut red number that Amy hadn't worn since college. "I'm free and easy?" He flipped through a few more outfits and pulled out one of the skirt suits her father liked her to wear to church meetings. "I hope you enjoy a challenge?"

"Are you even trying?" Amy asked.

"Hey, I like men. If you want to dress like a cowboy or a lumberjack, I know what gets me going. But this is sort of foreign territory."

Amy had a firm idea about the message she wanted to send. "I'm thinking the message of the day is, 'Do Not Enter,' like the road sign."

"Why did you make this date again?"

Not wanting to bore Holden with talks of mergers and money, she said, "Justice is a lawyer. He just kept talking until I agreed. I should probably call and cancel, but it seems rude to cancel at this point, and I guess I'm a sucker for a free meal."

"But not enough to go all the way?"

She threw a pillow at him. "Don't be gross."

"Gross? Some people enjoy the act of physical love."

"Ew."

"So, who's this Justice?"

She blushed. "Justice Labrador. The lawyer with the commercials." She was sure she didn't need to tell Holden which commercials.

He nodded. "Ah, yes. I might have just moved here, but I watch enough late-night TV to be familiar with him. It's hard to forget a lawyer whose commercials feature him barking at the judge like an angry dog." She could tell by the tone in his voice he disapproved of her dinner companion.

"We're going to the Jade Bowl. I've never been there before."

"Do you think he's anything like his commercials? When he's on a date, will he bark at your waiter?"

Amy sighed. "I hope not."

He nodded. "I'll pick a dark-colored top in case you want something with noodles in a thick sauce."

Amy couldn't decide whether to be grateful that he thought about stains or upset that he assumed she couldn't properly eat noodles. She couldn't, but that was beside the point. "Yeah, you're probably right."

He dug through her racks of clothes until he found a small clutch. "You can't take that big ass bag on a date either." He grabbed the handle of her purse, and the bottle of pepper spray fell out. He held it up. "Here's the pepper spray you were trying to find the other night." He looked at it again. "There's some residue on this." He sniffed the air, which admittedly still held a tiny hint of pepper. "Have you maced someone recently?"

She grabbed the mace away from him. "A lady never tells."

○ ○ ○

When Amy parked her old Honda outside Jade Bowl, between a gleaming new Lexus and a large Mercedes, she realized the place was a little more upscale than she'd expected. The weather was pleasant, and many people were drinking at the patio bar as she walked up to the door. One of them waved at her, and she recognized Justice Labrador.

He dressed well of course, being a lawyer pretty much required having a nice suit or two. He had accessorized with a gold silk tie decorated with little gavels, and the subdued lighting of the patio hid his unfortunate chin. He gave her a warm smile and stood as she approached the table. He took a step forward and held her hand, not a forceful masculine handshake, just an embrace and squeeze. "Amy, so nice to see you."

Despite his charisma, she couldn't help but remember he had coerced her into this dinner. "I'm here as you requested, or would that be commanded?"

"How about we stick to negotiated?" He actually circled around her and helped with her chair, which she found both cheesy and awkward.

Their waiter showed up to take drink orders. Justice ordered a cabernet, and she got her usual rum and Diet Coke.

When the waiter left, she said, "I was going to tell you no. You just left too quick for me to find a way to let you down easy."

Nodding, he said, "Yes, I admit, that was my strategy. It got you here, didn't it?"

She gave him her best glower. "Does this kind of manipulation work with other women? Do they find it cute?"

"Honestly," he said, "I've never tried it before. But I could tell you were going to say no, and I really wanted to have dinner with you."

"Did you consider the better choice would have been, you know, *not* having dinner with me?"

At that moment, David Graves walked over with Justice's wine and her rum and Diet Coke. She couldn't help but blurt out, "What the hell are you doing here?"

"And a pleasant evening to you, Ms. Love. Counselor." He nodded to Justice. "As a matter of fact, I own this establishment. I inherited it from my... mentor... Matt Rose, at the same time I took over Rosa. I decided to come here for dinner tonight since I ate at Rosa last night."

Amy sighed. "Why can't I get away from Calltelestar?"

Graves considered this for a moment. "Maybe we're all pawns in an eternal game between good and evil, and seemingly inconsequential coincidences are merely a physical manifestation of the unceasing struggle between celestial beings."

She didn't know whether he meant that as sarcasm or what, so she tried to get rid of him. "Actually, David, we're on a date—"

Before she could finish her statement, an absolutely gorgeous woman approached them. She wore a heavy leather jacket over a tight halter that revealed every curve, and her black jeans were so tight, they appeared to be painted on. Her hair was so dark, it didn't shine, but rather absorbed the light. Amy immediately felt jealous of her.

"David," the woman said, "who is this?" She glared daggers at Amy, apparently for being in a close proximity to David, as if she wasn't sitting with a date —and repulsed by her old boss.

"Raven, this is my former co-worker, America Love, and of course, you know Justice Labrador." He paused a moment to signal he was changing addressee. "Justice, Amy, this is my fiancée, Raven."

She held out her hand, and Justice took it like he was going to kiss it, but she pulled it back at the last minute. She looked down her perfect nose at him. "Mr. Labrador, you'll have to excuse the state of my nails. I was scheduled for a manicure today, but it didn't pan out." She shot Graves a look, probably some couple thing. "It's nice to meet you. I have, of course, seen your TV commercials."

He shrugged. "Don't hold them against me too much. I'm just trying to stir up some business."

She grinned. "Actually, I find them quite amusing. The midgets with the whips especially."

"Little people," Justice corrected.

Raven shrugged. How did she make a shrug look so sexy?

Feeling bad for Justice, Amy said, "Justice has done some excellent financial work on the merger."

Graves broke the awkward moment. "Well, enjoy your meal. Don't hesitate to speak with me if everything isn't to your satisfaction." He put his arm around Raven's shoulder. "Come along, dear."

Raven shrugged off his arm and stormed away. He smiled and followed her.

Once they were out of earshot, Amy said, "I can't stand that guy. And that fiancée, what a piece of work. Seriously, who calls themselves Raven? That's like the nickname a twelve-year-old boy would choose after playing too much *Dungeons and Dragons*."

Justice looked amused. "You sound like you don't know whether to be annoyed more by her or your former boss."

She involuntarily rolled her eyes. "Why not both? They're both connected to Calltelestar, and that place is evil."

"They are, you know, evil, technically. They're all Satanists."

"What? For real?" Amy had heard about Satanic cults before, but she thought all that talk was just religious paranoia or teenage boys trying to be edgy.

"Oh, yes. It's like the worst-kept secret among the Des Moines elites. The whole mess of them are a bunch of loony cultists. It's all bullshit, of course, good and evil, demons and angels fighting for supremacy."

Amy's head was spinning. "So, the Calltelestar people think..."

"They think they worship the Devil, and they have weird rituals in the basement of the Calltelestar building. They use it as a justification for their awful business practices."

Something occurred to her. "So, does the discrepancy between the share distribution in the merged company have anything to do with some kind of Satanic plot? Or maybe that proprietary software they're talking about has some kind of evil purpose?"

He nodded. "Now that you mention it, that kind of makes sense. How'd you figure that out?"

She sighed. "Well, I had some extra time in the office today, so I double checked your paperwork. The difference between the two companies' net worth seemed too large for the deal they were making 'proprietary technology' or not."Amy shook her head. "Between going to work for Tommy Norman, finding all this out, and certain other things, this has definitely been the weirdest week of my life."

"Certain other things," Justice repeated. "I can't believe dating 'The Law Dog' didn't even make the list."

She shook her head and chuckled at the invocation of his television persona. "Nope. You don't seriously think I'm impressed you're a lawyer? I grew up with lawyers. My father is a lawyer. My step-sister is a lawyer."

He snapped his fingers. "Darn, you aren't going to be impressed that I passed the Bar? Then I've got nothing going for me, no wit or intelligence or interesting anecdotes to amuse you, just the letters after my name."

She couldn't help smiling at this. "Well, at least you're honest. Besides, I think it's a fair assumption that if you had anything going for you, you wouldn't have to coerce an average girl like me into dating you. Unless... Good God, don't tell me you're infatuated with my sister from law school and dating me to ingratiate yourself to her."

"Wow." He leaned back and shook his head. "You have quite an imagination. First of all, you are far from average. I just thought that I'd like to have a nice meal with a pretty, intelligent woman. Maybe make a friend. And, God forbid, maybe we might like each other more than that."

Amy was about to call him out for empty flattery when the waiter came to take their order. Justice ordered some kind of weird fusion egg roll with curry chicken in it. Amy gave in to her small-town Iowa heritage and ordered pork chops, though at The Jade Bowl, they were marinated in a ginger sauce and came with fried rice.

Despite her inclination to argue with him for calling her smart and pretty, she decided to let it go and accept the compliment. "Flattery aside, without your coercion, I would not be going on a date with you. I have standards, and as much as I love my father, I don't want to date him. Hence, I have a no lawyer policy."

"When you use words like coerce and hence, you sound a bit like a lawyer yourself. You wouldn't date a lawyer, but if I quit and became a garbage man?"

"Probably not, because I don't like dating, but it wouldn't matter if you were a garbage man." She picked up her rum and coke and took a deep drink. "I probably wouldn't stick a garbage man with a big drinks bill."

"Well, I do deal with a lot of trash."

She guffawed into her glass, and rum and coke went up her nose.

A moment later, their food arrived, and they ate in silence for a few minutes.

"So," Justice asked, "how about this weather?"

"You know what?" Amy said, "I should just go. It's not even that I have a no lawyer policy as much as a no dating men policy."

Justice raised an eyebrow. "You mean, you usually date women?"

She shook her head. "No. I just don't really date. If there's anything I've learned about men in the last few years, it's that as long as he thinks there's a possibility of sex, he'll do or say anything, no matter now disingenuous."

He leaned forward and looked her in the eye. "Okay, then. I'll take it off the table. I promise I will never ask you for sex. If you ask me for it, demand me, beg me, I will say no."

"I'm willing to give you the benefit of the doubt, but you can't expect us to instantly become best friends, you'll just be in the 'trust but verify' zone."

"Is that similar to the 'friend zone' I keep hearing about? Because I'm told it's not a real thing, and I'm a sexist if I believe in it."

She nodded. "That's about right. 'Friend zone' implies you only see value in a relationship having a sexual component. It leaves no room for and gives no value to friendship."

"You seem to be implying that is the de facto outlook for males, and therefore I must advocate for it."

"I'm not accusing you of a viewpoint, per se. I'm simply stating I don't think a person should feel obligated to have sex with someone out of fear that they're being rude. Simple politeness or human kindness should be the default mode of discourse, not an implication of intimacy or a debt to be repaid. A quality friendship can be an admirable and desirable goal."

"Are you sure you're not a lawyer?"

She waved her blunt resturant knife at him. "Say that again, and I will cut you."

"Very well. After our date tonight, I will expect nothing but a firm handshake."

"That's a pretty high expectation. Do you wash your hands when you use the restroom?"

He smiled. "Of course. I'm not an animal."

"Consider your handshake imminent."

The rest of the evening went smoothly. Justice told her stories about court appearances, and she told him about the long list of jobs she'd attempted. They parted on good terms, and Justice did indeed get his handshake.

Later that evening, as she drifted off to sleep, Amy realized she'd enjoyed the evening. It was nice to talk to someone other than Holden. She still didn't know if she liked Justice. True to his word, he hadn't tried anything creepy during the date, but she felt like he'd tricked her into going in the first place. He might be quick witted and a little charming, but he also seemed a little untrustworthy. Maybe a lot untrustworthy.

7

Classifying the Succubus

The next day, Amy came into the office more or less on time. She sat down at her desk, and before she could check her email, she heard a loud knock through her wall. Worried Tommy might have fallen or hurt himself, she hurried around the corner and opened the door to Tommy's office.

Tommy was having sex with a very young girl up against the wall. They were going at it so hard he didn't even seem to notice she'd opened the door. Amy closed it slowly so she wouldn't make too much noise, but not before seeing another naked woman sprawled on the floor, apparently asleep. She made a mental note to always knock, although she doubted she'd ever come near his door again without having a flashback.

She tried to ignore the sounds of her boss having sex, as they continued for the entire rest of the morning. Finally, around noon, Tommy knocked on her door. Thankfully, he had put on his oversized jacket. "Oh, hello, Amy. I'm hoping I didn't disturb you this morning."

Amy shook her head. "Oh, no. Not at all," she said, despite feeling very disturbed.

"I started looking at Calltelestar's source code last night," he said as if this might explain things. Amy must have looked a little confused, so he continued. "You see, when I was in Bolivia, I met this biochemist. I hired her and opened a lab there, where we experimented with native plants."

"Uh huh." Amy still wasn't sure where this was going.

"Well, you see, the major cash crop there is the coca plant from which they derive cocaine."

Amy nodded, hoping he would stop sharing. He seemed to be a little manic however, speaking faster and louder than usual, his eyes darting back and forth
.

"Through careful experimentation on myself, my chemist mixed coca extract with MDPV, a chemical used in some psychoactive bath salts. It makes me really productive, giving me the ability to see things in the computer code that other people can't, but it gives me a lot of energy and makes me really horny. I sometimes need to have sex for eight or ten hours straight."

Amy nodded slowly as she wondered which was worse, seeing him in the act, or learning this new information. She wanted to throw up. After listening to his explanation, she felt entitled to a cleansing vomit.

"It's really powerful stuff. I call it B Sharp. I use it to see through the walls of reality and manipulate the underlying code. You should give it a try sometime."

Up until now, Amy had been nodding to show she understood his words and was paying attention. Now shook her head briskly. "No, thank you. I'll stick to al-cohol."

He rolled his eyes at her, which drew her attention to his pupils, which were huge. "Alcohol will kill you. This stuff is totally safe. Sure, it will raise your heart rate a bit, but that's just good cardio. My body's a tem-ple, you know." He flexed his bicep, the effect of which was lost in the folds of his oversized suit jacket.

Amy nodded mutely in response.

"We have a meeting at Calltelestar, be ready to leave around one."

Amy nodded again, still a bit speechless. However, she thought she should offer him one piece of advice be-fore they left. "Remember... Remember to put on pants, Mr. Norman." Thank God his over-sized jacket somewhat covered him. She'd still seen much more than she ever wanted to.

"Please, call me Tommy."

"Until you put on pants, I'd prefer to stay formal."

○ ○ ○

Amy insisted she should drive them to Calltelestar. She wasn't sure if Tommy would ever come down from the bath salt and cocaine concoction, but she surely wasn't going to ride in a car with him driving.

The drive to Calltelestar was a short one, so she didn't feel it necessary to make small talk. However, Tommy was chatty. "So, Amy, why did your father name you America anyway?"

"Patriotism, mostly."

"I find America's patriotism to be too severe, with giant flags everywhere. It's a little gauche, Amy."

"I don't know about that," Amy said, finding her-self in the awkward position of having to defend her fa-ther's patriotic attitude to her boss, despite her mixed feelings on loyalties determined by the location of one's birth. "It's okay for people to love their country."

"Patriotism and country are just imaginary con-
structs anyway, Amy. You should try this pharmaceutical I've invented. You would be able to see through all
these invented fabrications designed to aggrandize the
human ego. Realizing that you are just a piece of computer code can be... freeing."

"I already said I wouldn't try your experimental
drugs. I meant it the first time," she replied.

Amy had tried drugs a couple times in college,
and they'd made her feel queasy and disconnected
from the material universe. She had no desire to make
a habit of it. Also, in Tommy's case, the drug seemed to
be permanently loosening whatever grip he might have
had on reality.

"I'm perfectly happy with what I experience
now,"she said. "It's strange enough without coloring
outside the lines."

"Ah, but if I couldn't color outside those lines, I
wouldn't be able to make Calltelestar's code work," he
said. "I need to see through the threads of this reality
to pull them and shape them to my will." He mimicked
pulling threads from a tapestry, or maybe he thought
he was actually doing that.

"Um, we're here."

They were actually just pulling into the parking
lot, but Tommy opened the door anyway and leaned
out precariously.

"Please keep all doors closed until the vehicle
comes to a complete stop," Amy said.

Tommy closed the door and waited.

She parked Tommy's SUV and looked up at the
Calltelestar building. "That's odd," she said. If she'd
seen it a few weeks ago, she'd probably have thought
it was horrifying, but it had been a weird couple
weeks.

"What's odd?" Tommy asked.

"How there's a giant fiery pentagram hovering
above their building. I worked here not that long ago,
and I never noticed it before."

Tommy's eyebrows rose. "You can see it? Maybe you don't need any of my pharmaceuticals after all."

○ ○ ○

Amy felt weird, sitting in the Calltelestar People-connect lobby. The only other time she'd come in the front door of the building was on her first day of work. She hadn't even come here to interview. She'd applied online and interviewed with David Graves over the phone, a call that took about three minutes. When she'd started, she barely noticed the lobby was done in shades of gray. But she'd soon learned that everything else in the building was gray too.

At first, the gray had seemed innocuous, and she'd assumed that the color choice had been some kind of corporate attempt to look cool and neutral. However, as she had worked in the building, the lack of color had ground on her nerves. As hours ticked by, she had found herself wishing for more color than the environment would provide and wishing for a window in a way she never had before in an office environment.

Until she'd seen the giant pentagram outside, she had been ninety percent sure Justice Labrador was pulling her leg when he told her they were all a bunch of Satanists. She'd heard of the Satanic Panic in the 1980s, but hadn't that turned out to be a case of mass hysteria? If anything, it had shown that so-called Satanists weren't real. Still, the drab, gray decor could only be meant for soul sucking.

In addition to the spiritual attack of Calltelestar's decor, she had her stepsister sitting on her right and Tommy Norman, blitzed out of his mind on bath salts, sitting on her left. Tommy must have been coming down from his nightly binge though, as he now seemed spacey and inattentive, as if someone had hit his off switch.

Across the lobby, Dick Storm waited with Eric Driscoll, who already seemed pissed off at something.

111

Probably looking for a rematch with Graves. His face was still bruised from their encounter, and he was holding a cane—the ugly medical type, not a fashion accessory.

Amy and Tommy were the only ones not wearing suits. She was at least wearing a business casual top and slacks. Tommy wore a sport coat over knee-length tropical shorts and a Hawaiian shirt; apparently he still didn't feel like putting on pants.

One of the elevators behind the receptionist desk dinged, and David Graves emerged with Randy Clarke. Amy recognized Clarke from her time at Calltelestar. Strictly speaking, he never needed to come down to the call floors, but he seemed to enjoy leaving his penthouse office to sexually harass some of the younger female employees. He'd once stopped to give Amy an encouraging word, which had turned into a shoulder rub, which had turned into an offer to come back to his office and discuss "positions." Totally gross.

Clarke walked over to Storm. They shook hands and joked like they were the best of friends. Graves followed behind like a puppy, which gave Driscoll an opportunity for more targeted glaring. Driscoll stood, and Amy noticed him clench his jaw and lean heavily on the cane.

"Well, this is tense enough," Amy murmured.

"That's why Clarke is here," Debbie whispered. "He's showing Storm and Driscoll that Graves has the full support of the organization behind him. Though rumor says Clarke has fallen out of favor with the board."

Tommy let out a low whistle. "Am I the only one that can see their auras? Driscoll's is angry and Graves' is powerful, but Clarke and Storm, their auras are like twisted little goblins sitting on their shoulders."

Amy leaned over to Debbie and whispered, "He's on bath salts. Helps him write code."

Debbie gave a slight nod.

"So," Debbie asked, "how did your date with Justice go?"

"It wasn't a date," Amy replied, even though she knew it kind of had been.

"You let a man buy you food. Close enough. You know, you two would make a good couple. He might be a little rough around the edges now, with the struggling law practice and the silly commercials, but I'm sure he's going to make something of himself, not a Supreme Court justice, but something. He could do even better with a good woman."

Amy couldn't believe Debbie was talking like this. She was no one's good woman. "Well, why don't we find him one, then?"

"That's what I was trying to do. I know you're young, but eventually won't you want to settle down?"

"You're two years older than me. Don't you want to settle down?" Amy fired back.

Debbie didn't get a chance to answer because Clarke, Storm, and Driscoll started walking toward the elevators, and Graves walked over to them. He gave them his winning smile that made her almost forget that he'd physically attacked someone during their last meeting. "Hello, friends. We're going up to the top floor conference room. Follow me."

As the hired help, Amy, Debbie, and Tommy let the Calltelestar and Mediastorm executives go ahead and took a different elevator. Amy was not enthusiastic about being in an enclosed space with Graves and Driscoll glaring at each other. Come to think of it, why was she here again? Oh, yeah. God's will. Whatever that meant. If there really was a God, should she start going to church? She really preferred sleeping in on Sunday mornings.

With a ding, the elevator reached the top floor, and Amy realized that she'd been ruminating on the powers of good and evil instead of paying attention to her surroundings. Apparently, no one had noticed, especially her boss, who had either been staring into space or checking his reflection in the stainless-steel elevator wall.

They filed into a conference room already inhabited by the executive contingent. The seats were large and comfortable, but everything in the room was decorated in bland Calltelestar gray. Amy's eyes kept trying to refocus as it attempted to find the edge of things, like where the carpet ended and the wall started. The decor had to be specifically designed to make people feel hopelessness.

Randy Clarke shook Dick Storm's hand and then said, "I'll leave you in David's capable hands." As he was leaving the room, he took the opportunity to leer at Amy and Debbie. So creepy.

David Graves sat down at the head of the table. "So, how's everyone doing? Ready to make a lot of money?"

Storm crossed his arms. "I'm not convinced yet."

For a moment, everything was silent. If they had been in a teen movie, there would have been the sound effect of a record-scratch.

Graves stood up and leaned over the table. Amy flinched, afraid that he might lose his temper and hit someone again, or worse, stab them. "What? I thought we had a fucking deal."

Storm shrugged. "We haven't signed any papers yet. I'm not sure how much I trust you. Before we throw the two companies together completely, let's start with some baby steps. Maybe a joint venture."

The conference room phone buzzed.

Graves didn't look happy. He pointed aggressively at Storm. "To be continued..." He got up and pushed the intercom button. "Yes?"

"Mr. Graves, there's a Mr. Cunningham from the Department of Justice here to see you."

"Okay, thanks." He pushed a button to end the call.

Before Amy knew what was going on, Storm had pulled a gun from inside his jacket.

Graves pulled a huge handgun from one side of his suit and his big, wicked looking dagger from the other "What the fuck, Storm?"

Before Graves was done talking, Eric Driscoll pulled a similarly giant handgun from under his jacket and aimed it back at Graves. Tommy lazily took two guns out of his jacket and pointed them at both men. Amy shot him a puzzled look. "Why did you bring guns? You are high as fuck."

He shrugged. "I thought something like this might happen, and I didn't want to be left out."

Amy considered accusing them of another dick-measuring contest, but it probably wouldn't work twice, and with the number of guns in play, she would only be stating the obvious.

"Gentlemen," Debbie snapped in her most over-bearing-bitch-from-hell voice, "put away your pistols. The Justice Department works with the Federal Trade Commission to oversee all mergers. In case we ulti-mately do decide to go ahead with this merger, we still need their rubber stamp. I invited Agent Cunningham, who oversees antitrust issues for Media and Entertain-ment from the Chicago Field Office, as he was in town for another meeting. He's not a cop, he's just an ac-countant with a badge." She made lowering hand signs. She gave David Graves a pointed look. "I told you about this, Mr. Graves."

Graves smiled mischievously, like a little kid who'd just gotten caught stealing a cookie. He put away his gun and dagger. "Yeah, I knew he was com-ing. Just keeping people on their toes."

Storm followed his example and put away his guns. Driscoll reluctantly followed his example.

Amy looked over at Tommy. "Guns away, please." She was genuinely worried he would shoot someone out of paranoia or hallucination.

"Oh, oh yeah." He put his guns away. "Forgot I took them out."

Amy sighed. Just like the pants situation earlier.

Once satisfied no one was about to get murdered, Debbie said, "Mr. Graves, could you have Agent Cunningham brought up to the conference room?"

Graves picked up the phone and relayed the request to someone. They waited in awkward silence until a skinny, blonde woman with scaly, green skin led a middle-aged man wearing a similarly middle-aged suit into the room.

"Holy shit," Amy whispered to Tommy. "What's wrong with her skin?"

"Oh, you can see it too? She's a demon. Probably a succubus," Tommy replied casually.

Amy didn't know whether to believe him or not. Her boss was bombed out of his mind, but she had met an angel. Plus, that skin tone did not belong to anything classified as mammalian despite ample possession of the requisite glands. "Why doesn't the fed notice?"

"Most people see what they expect to see, especially if they haven't had my special pharmaceutical. But how can you see her true form? Have you been borrowing from my stash?"

Amy shrugged. She suspected it had something to do with being a holy warrior or hanging out with angels, but she really didn't want to confess that in her present company.

Agent Cunningham was speaking with his demon escort. "Thank you for accompanying me, Ms...?"

"Julia," she purred. "It was my pleasure." She ran her hand down the agent's arm in a way that repulsed Amy. He reluctantly turned to the conference table.

Debbie stood. "Agent Cunningham, welcome to Calltelestar Peopleconnect. Have a seat. I'm Debbie Sutter. We spoke on the phone. And let me introduce David Graves, who is handling the Calltelestar side of things, Dick Storm of MediaStorm..." She went around the table, introducing everyone there. Amy was given the title, "Mr. Norman's associate."

116

Once they were introduced, Cunningham glared at Tommy. "I have your anti-virus software on my computer. It's always asking me to upgrade it or run some kind of update."

"Oh hello, agent." Tommy shrugged. "I haven't had anything to do with that software for years. Intel bought it from me. You'll have to take it up with them."

Realizing he wasn't going to get anything more than that from Tommy, Cunningham scowled and got down to business. "So, Calltelestar Peopleconnect wants to merge with MediaStorm into a shiny new company. Exciting times, ladies and gentlemen."

"Have you had a chance to look over the financials?"

The agent nodded. "Yes, I have. And I think you make a good case for the merger not violating any anti-trust laws. There's just one little thing missing."

Debbie looked shocked. "I'm not sure I understand. I had a contractor supply the data, but I double checked it all."

Graves smiled. "I'm sure we can come up with some special consideration to solve our problem."

Nodding, Tommy pulled out both of his guns and pointed them at Agent Cunningham. "Do you want me to waste him?"

Graves slapped the table, and Agent Cunningham jumped about a foot into the air.

"Calm down, Tommy." Graves growled. "He just wants a bribe."

"It would be cheaper to shoot him," Tommy said unhelpfully.

Amy casually reached over and put her arm across Tommy's forearms. She pressed down, lowering his guns.

He looked back at Cunningham, "And I'm guessing your price just went up."

Cunningham shrugged trying to look nonchalant, but obviously riled by Tommy's guns. "Bribe is such a dirty word. I'm simply retiring from the DOJ in a few months, and I could use a job afterward."

Graves smiled. "Oh, I don't think that would be a problem at all. You're exactly the kind of person we like here at Calltelestar. I think we could find an advisory position, six figure salary, low responsibility, guaranteed ten years employment, that kind of thing. You could even work from home if you wanted to stay in Chicago. Of course, you'll have to sign our standard employment contract."

Cunningham smiled. "Well, now that we all know the score, I'm going to recommend we fast-track this merger."

Graves smiled, stood, and walked around the table. "Congratulations on your new job, Mr. Cunningham." They shook hands like old friends.

"Well," Cunningham said, "That concludes my business here." He seemed overjoyed, like he hadn't expected things to go so easily.

"Believe me, the pleasure was all mine. Julia should be waiting just outside. Perhaps she could give you a tour of Des Moines. The famous Iowa State Fair is going on. Have you ever had deep fried butter?"

Cunningham nodded. "Interesting. I'm sure we can find something to do."

"Welcome to the family." Graves patted him on the shoulder, and Cunningham left.

Graves turned to the groups. "So, now that we're done with that moron, who's ready for a merger?"

Amy couldn't help but interrupt. "Did you just bribe a federal agent?"

Graves yawned. "No, I promised to bribe a federal agent, a handshake deal. I didn't write him a check. Besides, once Julia is done with him, he won't have much will of his own anyway."

Dick Storm let out a low chuckle. "You bastard," he said appreciatively. "What made you think to bring in a succubus?"

"Well, she does work here, and she does enjoy destroying the occasional man when she's not busy doing the HR paperwork." Graves returned to his seat. "Now, what do we have left? Anything on the legal side?"

Debbie shook her head. "We're putting together the last of the contracts. Once Agent Cunningham puts together our DOJ approval, we'll be ready to go."

"Storm?" Graves asked.

Storm shook his head. "As I said earlier, I'm still not sold. A week ago, sure, I would have happily moved forward, but I'm not sure I want to do business with Calltelestar anymore."

Graves looked shocked. "I just offered a million-dollar bribe to a federal official. Surely that shows good faith."

"So what? You probably aren't going to have to pay him anyway after that succubus sucks out his will. Even if he escapes her, are you that gun shy at putting up a million over ten years?"

Graves scowled. "No, we're good for it, but why your sudden indecision?"

Storm leaned back in his chair. "Let's just say that the other night, I was accosted by a MediaStorm subscriber in the parking lot of my office. My company had treated him so poorly that he was willing attack me at gunpoint, over cable. When I think of all the bad work I've done, I'm afraid that your bureaucratic temperaments might not be a good fit for my company."

"So," Tommy asked, "where does that leave the merger, eh? Are you leaving the deal?"

Storm raised his hand and made a so-so gesture. "Let's just say I'm not ready to let Calltelestar get into my panties yet. Maybe take me out on a date or two. Show a girl a good time." Amy didn't know whether to be disgusted by the old man's analogy or to wonder if he actually was wearing panties.

Graves sighed. "So, what do you propose?"

"I thought we could go in on a much smaller joint venture, to see if we really want to be in bed together." Storm nodded to Eric, who took a stack of folders from his briefcase and passed them around the table. "This is the movie, *Karma*, written and directed a decade ago by Jason Sizemore. Currently, it is owned by Spencer Rich."

"I thought they liquidated The Rich Company after all those rape allegations came out," Graves said.

Storm nodded. "Yes, they liquidated the company, but Rich bought *Karma* with his personal money. He's low on cash now and desperate to sell the property, but none of his old Hollywood cronies will take a meeting with him. He's willing to sell to us for three million dollars. Next year is the tenth anniversary of the release, and we can make that back in streaming rights. We'll double our money over the next three years."

While he had been talking, Tommy had paged through his folder. He flipped it shut and said, "I'm a little confused. We were merging the company, but now we're doing a movie thing?"

Amy nodded to Tommy. Given the drugs in his system, she was impressed he'd followed along that well. She spoke slowly. "Yes, Tommy. They may still do the merger, but they want to try this movie deal first. The merger is just postponed. They want to get to know each other better."

"And where am I in all of this? You don't need any software written. Am I out of the deal?" Stoned or not, the man knew how to protect his monetary interests.

Storm looked at Graves. "What do you say, should we cut him in for his twelve percent if he can cover that part of the action?"

Graves nodded. "Fine by me. It would be a nice good-faith gesture."

Tommy didn't look especially happy about having to give up... Amy stopped to do the math. Twelve percent of a million dollars was $120,000, so twelve percent of three million must be $360,000, probably not that much money for Tommy Norman, and a drop in the bucket from what he might earn if the merger went through.

Despite the cost of buying in, Tommy nodded. "Sure. I'll put up my share."

"So, Debbie," Storm said, "you ready to go out to California to negotiate this deal? I made an appointment with Rich for Friday evening."

Debbie shook her head. "I'm sorry. I need to be in the courthouse all day on Friday. I have time sensitive filings that have to be made in person to the clerk of court and documents that need to be witnessed by a judge." She looked over at Amy. "Why don't you have Amy do it?"

"What?" Amy blurted out. "Why would you want me to negotiate with the sex offender?"

"*Alleged* sex offender," Storm corrected.

Debbie continued. "Amy knows everyone involved in this deal, and she was practically running our father's law office from the time she was fourteen until she left for college. She likes to pretend to be a slacker, but she's probably negotiated as many contracts as I have, and she knows as much about intellectual property ownership as I do."

"But..." Amy tried to think of a way to protest. She really didn't want to have to sit on a plane for hours to talk to Spencer Rich—the man was creepy.

"Sounds like a great idea to me," Graves said. "I'm sure Amy can handle it."

8

A Touch of Satan

After the meeting, Amy made sure that Tommy was on his office couch, sleeping off whatever drugs he had taken. He was also alone. Thankfully, Tommy's 'female companions' had already woken up and left the building.

Her duties done, Amy left work, stopped at the grocery store, and then drove home. She parked in the dark parking lot behind her apartment building. The security light was out, so she sat in her car for a minute looking through her purse, making sure her apartment keys and pepper spray were both within easy reach. When that was done, she opened her car door and stepped out.

Her groceries were in the back seat, so she turned to open the back door and leaned in to get the bags.

Unseen hands grabbed her, pulling her out of the car, pulling her out of the car by her hair. She tried to fight, but the guy was behind her, and his grip on her was solid.

Her attacker slammed her against the hood of her car, and reached under her to grope her left breast.

"I bet you didn't think you'd see me again, did you, bitch? This time, you won't have your little fag cop to help you."

Amy knew the voice. It was Nelson, the guy who had tried to attack her outside the bar the night she'd met Holden. He'd come back for revenge. How had he found her? Was he stalking her just because his ego had been bruised?

Amy felt a tingling in the back of her head, which quickly spread to the rest of her body. At first, she thought she might be having a panic attack, but then she realized she was making a fist. She wanted to fight this horrible man, to hurt him. She took a deep breath, preparing herself.

Nelson's grip loosened, and he let out a wail.

Amy turned to find David Graves hoisting Nelson off the ground by his underpants. He'd grabbed them out of the back of Nelson's jeans and now had them stretched a good three feet beyond their initial dimensions. He gave another tug, lifting Nelson's feet off the ground. The waistband reached the back of Nelson's head before tearing free.

Nelson dropped back to his feet, but before he could regain his balance, Graves tossed the remains of the underpants aside and pushed Nelson's face into the hood of the car where a few moments ago, Nelson had held Amy.

Graves smiled at her. "Friend of yours?"

She shook her head. "No!"

"Well in that *case*." He banged Nelson's head into the car for emphasis. "You better *learn*." *Bang*. "To leave the *lady. Alone.*" *Bang. Bang.* He held Nelson up by his shirt collar and said, "Apologize to the lady."

Nelson said nothing, as Graves had beaten him unconscious.

For a moment, Amy was speechless at Graves's violent display. Finally, she said the first thing that popped into her head. "You dented my car."

Looking at the Nelson's forehead-shaped dent in the top of her fender, Graves frowned and said, "Sorry." He dropped Nelson face-first on top of the torn underwear. "What's up with this guy?"

Amy frowned. "Just some jerk I met at the bar a couple weeks ago. I never thought I'd see him again. Apparently, he didn't like the beating he'd gotten then." She didn't bother to add that Holden had done the actual beating. She didn't want to sound soft.

"You should be more careful who you hang out with," Graves said. "Want to get a drink?"

Amy thought about giving him her standard speech about not expecting a sexual relationship in exchange for common courtesy, but she was feeling a little queasy. "Actually, I..." She stumbled and Graves caught her.

"Whoa there. Why don't I take you up to your apartment and make sure you don't have a concussion or anything?"

"Sounds good. Grab my groceries from the back seat, would you?"

Graves grabbed the grocery bag out of her car. "There's nothing in here but a huge bottle of rum, a two liter of Diet Coke, and a bag of Cheetos."

"I didn't want to carry a bunch of food up the stairs."

Graves helped her up the stairs to her apartment as if she weighed no more than a feather. As she was opening her door, Raquel popped out from her apartment. "Hi, Amy. Everything all right here?"

"Yes. Well, no. Some asshole jumped me in the parking lot, and David helped me out. Don't worry, he's a work friend, so he's safe enough, I guess." Amy kind of wondered if this was true. He had just saved her from an assault and maybe worse, but he also was an evil Satanist who had just beaten a man unconscious. It had been on her behalf though, so she decided to give him the benefit of doubt. She needed to find out why he was lurking in her parking lot.

"Okay, sweetie. Just yell if you need anything," she said pointedly. She looked David in the eye. "I can hear everything through these walls," she said and closed her apartment door.

When Amy managed to unlock the door, Graves half-carried her inside and sat her down on the bed. He walked into the kitchen with her grocery bag and shortly returned with two tall rum and Diet Cokes. He handed her one and grabbed the chair from her dressing table. He pulled it up and offered to clink glasses with her. They clinked.

David got up in her face and gazed deeply into her eyes.

"What are you doing?"

"Looking to see if your eyes are dilated. Do you have a headache?"

She shook her head no, which made the room spin just a little. "No, just dizzy."

He nodded. "I'm not a nurse, but I'm going to assume you'll live."

"What would you have done if you thought I had a concussion?"

"Probably take your drink away."

She took a deep drink. "Lucky I meet your seal of approval."

"I bet you're wondering why I was lurking in your parking lot," he said.

She nodded. "At the risk of seeming ungrateful for my rescue, yes. I was even planning to use the word lurking."

"I wanted to clear the air. I've been watching you the last week or so. You're doing an admirable job putting up with Tommy Norman, and I think you actually know what's going on as far as this merger is concerned. I fired you from Calltelestar, and I thought you might like an explanation why. I don't usually get to talk to people after the fact. I think you noticed how Eric reacted to seeing me again." He gulped his drink, draining an amount of rum and Diet Coke that would have gotten Amy quite drunk, now that she had a baby liver.

Amy sometimes wondered if she should ask for her old liver back, but her parents had raised her to be gracious about gifts, even ones she didn't want. As a plus, she had to admit getting drunk was a lot cheaper now, and she would probably live a little longer, so she had that going for her.

Graves made a face at his drink. "Not the same without regular Coke."

"Calories. It's this or exercise." She took a sip of her drink. "You said you fired me because of my stepmother."

He shrugged. "That is what I told you."

"She didn't bribe you then?"

"Oh, yes. She did, and I took her money. I didn't spend it on Scotch, though. I already have a ton of Scotch. So technically, yes, your stepmother bribed me, and I fired you, but those things were only loosely related. She got me to notice you, and once I took a close look at you, I realized you had a good soul."

"A what now?"

"You see, Amy. I'm what some people might call a dark wizard."

Amy had absolutely no idea how to respond to this, so she didn't. She just waited for him to explain.

"You know about Satanists, right? Not that LaVey 'Church of Satan' stuff, but the real, dark, worshiping the Devil stuff?"

"I thought that was all just a myth," She lied.

"And people work really hard to keep you believing that. People like my bosses, Randy Clarke and Charlie Stevens. You see, they tricked me into joining their Satan-worshiping club, and now they own my soul. Want me to refresh that?"

Amy realized she had finished her drink already. She knew she shouldn't drink more, but she passed her glass over to Graves, who took it into the kitchen and returned with it full.

"So..." She could already hear the slur in her words. "Why are you telling me this?"

"I fired you from Calltelestar because I read your aura. I could tell you were good. I didn't want them to corrupt you." He sighed. "I used to be a good person. I didn't want them to ruin you too."

"Holy shit. And what does this have to do with sending me to California to negotiate a movie deal?"

He shrugged. "Nothing. I just thought you'd be good at it." He paused and studied her face. "You don't believe me, about being a good person, do you?"

Amy considered for a moment. "No, I actually do. You really sound sincere. Shit, Graves. You're so good at being an evil asshole, I never even stopped to consider you didn't enjoy it."

"I used to be really nice. I had a girlfriend who hated me for it. Everyone thought I was a real loser. Then one day, I flipped out and attacked Matt Rose. I thought he was going to fire me, but he promoted me. Little did I know that when I signed on as an executive, I also signed away my soul."

"Fuck you, Graves."

"What?"

"You made me feel sorry for you, you fucking fucker."

○ ○ ○

At work the next day, Amy got a text from Justice. "Want to come over and drink some wine?"

She could definitely use a drink, but she didn't want him to think it was a date. "Sure, can I bring a friend?"

128

She waited for a response, and waited more, wondering if she'd caught him off guard or there was a glitch in the texting system. "Sure," the response finally came, followed by an address.

She sent a text to Holden. "Hey, want some free booze from the Iowa Law Dog?"

Again, the response was not quick. She sent another text. "Well?"

A moment later, she got, "Thinking."

"Oh, come on. Free wine. Plus, I need a wingman." She sent the address.

He sent back, "Okay, but drive home, and I'll pick you up. I know how you drink, and I don't want you driving after."

Amy followed Holden's instructions and drove home. She didn't want to have an argument about her drinking, as she couldn't exactly explain that an angel had put some kind of miracle on her.

When he picked her up in his Miata, she noticed he was wearing a t-shirt emblazoned with a large badge, reading "Phoenix Regional Police Academy." It was the first time she had ever seen him in a regular, printed t-shirt, and she couldn't help but comment, "Subtle."

"I just want to point out to Mr. Labrador that police officers are people too."

"Yeah, I think I read that somewhere."

"Very cute," he said, matching her attitude.

"Thank you," Amy said, striking a pose and pretending to misunderstand his sarcasm for a compliment on her outfit. "But seriously, Justice has been really nice to me. I don't think he really has anything against cops. It's just a marketing thing."

"I still don't have to like him." Changing the subject, he asked, "How's the new job going?"

"I got to witness the bribery of a federal official."

"Forget I asked. I don't want to know."

They rode in silence the rest of the way. Amy couldn't help but wonder if their young relationship was starting to strain, him being in law enforcement and her working for evil men.

Justice Labrador's law office might have been a modest law practice, but he had a nice-sized house in a gated community, which was probably why he was desperate for money. The style was cold and modern. As he welcomed them inside, she saw the interior of the house was nicely decorated with warm colors which seemed to apologize for the exterior.

He handed each of them a glass of white wine. "Some people say you should start with whites and then make your way through the heavier reds. Other people say you should start with reds and move to crisper whites. Wine is not an exact science." He walked them to the living room. "I'm going to start with a sweet white. This first wine is a Gewurztraminer, which you may be able to tell from the length of the name is German."

Amy realized Holden was gazing into the void that was Justice's chin. "Um, Justice, I should have introduced you. This is my friend, and nearly neighbor, Holden."

"Nearly neighbor," Justice asked, "How does that work?"

"I'm in the same apartment complex, just two buildings down the street," Holden explained.

"Nice." Justice paused. "So are you two..."

"Just good friends," Holden answered.

After that, they made small talk until the wine had marinated them a little. Once again, Amy felt herself losing control more than usual. Eventually, she said something guaranteed to piss off everyone in the room. "So, Justice, Holden hates your commercials."

Justice nodded. "I had noticed the shirt, and I was wondering if you wore it on purpose, Holden. I know the commercials lay it on a little thick. But I am primarily a criminal defense attorney, and while I have nothing but respect for the members of law enforcement, my clients have quite a different opinion. Those ads might be offensive, but they bring in the business. Honestly, I blame that show *Breaking Bad*. Everyone wants a crooked attorney these days. They think we can do something magic and side-step the law without getting disbarred."

"Not to mention making you enough to live in a big, fancy house," Holden added.

Justice shrugged. "I got a good deal. Neo-modern residential has gone out of style, and the place needed work. Once you get into a certain price range, having last year's kitchen cabinets can knock a lot off the price, even for people who don't do their own cooking. So far, I've only redone this main room and my bedroom. The other rooms are done in a style best described as 'late nineteen-eighties swinger party.' And no, I'm not going to show them to you."

Amy actually liked Justice's style, it was colorful without being garish, eclectic without seeming mismatched, and there was no hint of beige. "It's amazing. Did you do it yourself, or did you get a decorator?"

"I hired a general contractor who had a good eye for detail. We chose everything together."

Amy nodded. "I'd really like to see the bedroom." Then she blushed. "To see your renovation."

She braced herself for some kind of innuendo, but Justice just smiled. "Sure, but I have to warn you, I might have left some dirty underwear on the floor."

Holden put down his wineglass. "I'll watch my step."

After a tour of the bedroom, they returned to the living room. Amy was starting to feel more than a bit tipsy. "So, Justice, would you work for Calltelestar if you didn't have this big house to pay for?"

"Well, as I said, it wasn't that expensive. It's one of the smaller houses in the area and it's a bit run down. You should go a couple blocks north of here. That's the neighborhood David Graves lives in."

"Oh, I didn't know he lived around here," Amy said.

131

"Yes, he actually inherited the house from his mentor, Matt Rose. They say Graves beat him to death with a framing hammer."

"That's got to be a rumor though, right?" Amy said. "I heard rumors at Calltelestar, but he actually killed a man? Why isn't he in prison?"

Holden rolled his eyes. "Oh, innocent Amy. Murderers go free all the time. We don't like it, but the police aren't omniscient." He drained his wine glass. "Mind if I kill the bottle?" He picked it up without waiting for Justice's answer.

"Sure," Justice responded. "You see, Amy. It's a longstanding tradition among Satanists—"

"Wait," Holden said, "Calltelestar is full of Satanists? Like the LaVey type or the really dark stuff?"

"The really dark stuff," Justice said. "As I was saying, it's a longstanding tradition among Satanists. If they kill one of their own in a duel, they inherit their foe's possessions. They're a bit like vampires that way."

Amy felt the blood drain from her face. "Like what?"

Justice shook his head and quickly said, "Like on that TV show. You know. What's the name of it? I think it's on that vampire movie channel." He seemed nervous.

"I don't get that channel. Is that even a channel?" Amy asked.

Justice shrugged. "Never mind. Maybe I dreamed it. These days, the victor usually gives up their claim and lets the next-of-kin inherit, but Rose had no close relatives."

"But that can't even be remotely legal," Amy argued.

"Legal-ish," Justice said. "Paperwork can be backdated, signatures forged."

Amy knew a thing or two about the law. "They'd have to get a lawyer to do that. Didn't you just say they'd get disbarred if they got caught?"

"Yes, but the Satanists pay extremely well, they know how to bribe a judge, and it's almost only done when there is no one to contest the phony will."

Holden added, "I'm sure they have powerful people inside their fold as well."

"Quite right," Justice agreed.

"Wait," Amy said. "Are you...? Oh, my God, what about Debbie?"

Justice shook his head. "No for me, and not as far as I know for Debbie. I think they wanted a neutral third party for the merger."

"What about Tommy Norman?"

He shook his head again. "No, I don't think so. Tommy Norman is a lot of things, but I don't think he actually worships Satan. Works for, yes, but worship, probably not. They brought him into the deal because of Calltelestar's software."

"Really?" Amy still didn't understand why some software package was so ineffable and all-important, but they talked about it like it was more important than the money or the companies.

Justice lowered his voice, as if they were in public and not in his living room. "I'm not supposed to tell you this. I'm not even supposed to know, but Graves let it slip. Calltelestar's software sacrifices people to Satan."

Amy couldn't wrap her head around this. "What the fuck? It's software. How does that work?"

"It's something to do with annoying people on the phone. Say you get a call from a telemarketer, and you don't hang up right away. You haven't lost your life, but you've lost five minutes of your life, a very tiny percent of your life. Well, if they have a thousand employees calling a hundred people a day..."

Amy finished his sentence. "It's like they sacrifice a life to Satan every day."

Justice nodded. "Maybe not every day, but every few months. Now, extend that to cable and Internet. A lower number of people reached, but many of them spending hours every day, watching reality television, binge streaming, Facebooking, flame warring."

Amy's mouth dropped open. "Holy shit."

"That's it," Holden said. "We're going to have to get an Uber home. I'm way too sober for this conversation." He poured himself another generous portion of wine. "If I black out, though, you have to remind me to cancel my cable tomorrow."

Amy frowned. "You'll have to remember yourself. I have to fly to Los Angeles tomorrow."

○ ○ ○

Amy didn't like to think of herself as a nervous person, but she was nervous now. She'd rented a car at the airport—a Ford Mustang; her father would approve—and spent two perilous hours navigating the LA freeway system, which made Des Moines traffic look like an amusement park kid's ride.

Now she was driving up a narrow, winding road into the Hollywood hills. Occasionally, she passed a secluded gate with a keypad and speaker box. Finally, her GPS told her she'd arrived at her destination. She stopped the car and looked around. She'd gone just past a driveway. Squinting down the path, she saw a metal arch with the house number she was looking for. She did a three-point turn and pulled up to the speaker.

A few moments after she pressed the call button, a gruff voice answered, one she'd heard once over the telephone and on a handful of interviews on YouTube. "Mr. Rich. This is Amy Love. Debbie Sutter arranged our meeting. I'm here to discuss the sale of *Karma*."

Amy didn't like any of this. Why couldn't they have done the negotiation over the phone, perhaps with Rich's lawyers, or at least in a public place? She didn't want to meet face-to-face with a man blackballed from Hollywood for sexually molesting some of the most famous women in the world.

"Who? I'm expecting some girl named America."

Amy sighed. "Yes, my name is America. But you can call me Amy."

With a buzz, the gate slowly swung open, and Amy drove the Mustang up a twisting path through increasingly extravagant landscaping. The house itself was impressive, around the size of a Holiday Inn Express, and unfortunately just as blocky in its appearance, but with much more expensive-looking statuary. She parked the car under the *porte cochere* and walked up to the front door.

Before she had time to knock, Spencer Rich himself answered the front door. Did he not have any staff? Had they all quit because of the scandal? He could surely still afford someone to answer the door. He might have sold some of his other houses, but he was hardly poor.

"Welcome to Hollywood, Ms. Love." He seemed to be wearing nothing but a very short robe, not a good sign, and she kept her eyes north, lest something peek out the bottom.

"I'm sorry, did I catch you um..." She tried to think of something non-sexy involving less clothing. "...exercising?"

"No, I was just lounging around the house. I just opened a bottle of *Cristal*. Would you care to join me in a glass of Champagne?"

"Oh, I suppose so." She might not trust him as far as she could throw him, but she also didn't want to sound too aloof going into a negotiation. Besides, she was not going to turn down alcohol that expensive, as she was ninety-nine percent sure he wasn't going to drug her before they signed the contracts.

He nodded. "Wonderful. Follow me."

They walked from the vestibule into a room with thirty-foot ceilings, probably meant for hosting parties of a few hundred people. Despite the house's blockiness and the size of the room, the decorating managed to make it look warm and inviting. The back wall was entirely glass, overlooking the city. The side walls were covered in large paintings, and items with little plaques underneath them. The centerpiece of the collection seemed to be a large *Gone with the Wind* poster signed by several cast members. Overstuffed furniture sat round the room's perimeter, making conversation nooks. Rich led her to the corner of the room towards a staircase.

"Um, where are we going exactly?" Amy asked.

"The *Cristal* is in my bedroom," he answered.

Amy revised her chances of getting drugged and raped up to seventy percent. "In that case, why don't we just sit here and get our negotiations out of the way?" Because she didn't care how much faith the team had in her, her body was not part of the negotiation.

"So, you won't come to my bedroom then?"

She shook her head. "No. I am here to represent my clients, and that is all."

He looked confused. "But then why did they send me a stripper?"

"What? Me?" In what way did she look like a stripper? She was wearing a pantsuit wrinkled from five hours on an airplane and two in a car. She'd touched up her makeup in the airport bathroom, but she probably looked like hell.

"Your name is 'America Love.' That's got to be a stripper name."

Amy said a silent thank you to her father. "Well, Mr. Rich, that happens to be my name, and I am not a stripper, that is just the name my father gave me. I like to think when he was looking at his newly born baby girl, he wasn't thinking about strippers."

He sighed. "Very well." He waved at a nearby conversation nook. "Please, have a seat." He plopped down on a couch, and his robe rode up a couple inches, revealing he was indeed naked underneath.

Being extra careful not to accidentally glance at his wrinkly, old balls, and perhaps give him some encouragement, Amy sat down gingerly and said, "Look,

let's get down to business, so you can get back to..."
What had he been doing, drinking Champagne in the
nude? "...whatever you were doing before I got here.
You have a property, *Karma*. We're interested. I'm prepared to offer you two point two million." She was au-
thorized to go all the way to three million, but there
was no reason to put her best offer on the table right
away. It wouldn't hurt if she could take off a few hundred thousand, maybe they'd give her a bonus.

Rich shook his head. "No. I don't think so."

"What is your counteroffer, if you don't mind me
asking?"

"All the paperwork for *Karma* is in my bedroom,
and I'll consider making a counteroffer if you come upstairs with me."

She shook her head. "I am here to buy a movie,
not to be your plaything, Mr. Rich. Either talk business,
or I will leave." Sure, there was a chance she might get
fired, but she trusted her ability to find another job
more than she trusted Rich to keep his robe on.

Rich sighed and gave her a condescending look.
"Look, I'm a man who's used to getting what he wants.
I have something you want, and you have something I
want. Why make things this hard? The fewer clothes
you're wearing, the easier I'll be to negotiate with."

Amy was left momentarily speechless, wondering
how to remain civil and one-up him in their verbal spar-
ring match. Nothing came to mind. "Look, jackass, I'm
here to deal, so either make a counteroffer, or thanks
for wasting my time and making me come all the way
from Iowa."

He sighed. "Damn political correctness. Well, with
that attitude, I'm not going to let you have *Karma*, but
we might be able to offer you a different property."

She shook her head. "No. I'm here to negotiate for
Karma. I'm offering two point two million. Now take it
or leave it."

Rich stood up, neglecting to adjust is robe, and
started to walk toward her. "Look, I'm not a bad guy.

I'm just looking for a little *quid pro quo.* I could be a powerful friend to you. I still know a lot of people in the industry."

Amy stood and backed away from him. "Mr. Rich, this is a bad idea. It's never going to happen. You're just throwing away a lot of money."

"Trust me, sweetie," Rich said, continuing to reach for her. "You'll feel better once things get started. I know, some girls just need a little time to warm up."

Amy started to feel the tingling sensation in the back of her head again, the one she'd felt when Nelson had attacked her. This time however, she didn't have Graves to come save her. The tingling spread all over her body, and her heart felt like it was going to explode. She backed into a wall.

Rich walked over and leaned into her like he was going to kiss her.

Her body buzzing with power, Amy reached behind her, and her hand closed on something. She brought it around and held it to Rich's throat. It was a sword.

She glanced over, and there was a little plaque on the wall. "Sword used by Douglas Fairbanks, *The Mark of Zorro,* 1920."

Rich took a few steps back, and Amy held the sword out, pointing directly at his throat. "Mr. Rich, I came here to negotiate a deal on a film, *Karma.* Are you going to make me a counteroffer?"

"I can't," he whined.

She lowered the sword to his groin. "Either bargain in good faith, or I'm going to cut your fucking cock off."

"You can't do that. My lawyers will ruin you."

She rolled her eyes. "Oh, yes, I'll be in a lot of trouble, and you won't have a dick. Now, agree to my offer or make me a counter."

"I can't give you the film. I already sold it."

Amy felt like she'd been slapped, all that work just to find out this idiot didn't even own the film.

"I own a few more films. I'll sell you something else."

She shook her head. "Okay. I'll let you show me some options, but first, I'm going to leave, and in an hour, we can meet in a public place, somewhere pants are required."

"I can't make a deal like that in public. Everyone will know I'm low on cash."

"Tough shit." She flicked the sword at him. "Also, I'm keeping this."

"That sword's worth a lot of money!"

"I'm sure it is. Consider it an asshole tax."

Three hours later, she had a deal. It wasn't for the movie she'd originally expected to buy, but her clothes had stayed on. The deal was a good one, and everyone was bound to be pleased. Plus, she had acquired a genuine piece of Hollywood memorabilia.

As she drove down back to the airport, she mentally kicked herself. She should have gotten the little plaque to go with the sword.

Her phone rang. It was Holden. She put it on speaker. "Hey, Holden, what's up?"

"Just making sure you're okay. Did Rich try to mess with you at all?"

"Oh, he did. He threw himself at me. I had to fight him off."

"Did you manage to get away? Did he hurt you?"

Amy chuckled. "I think I managed quite well. In fact, I got you a souvenir. Do you like swords?"

9

Devil Daze

Amy waited outside her apartment. They had another meeting about the merger, and Tommy said he would pick her up. Since he was driving, she had been quite adamant about him abstaining from bath salts before taking the meeting.

Thankfully, he showed up on time, tired but sober.

Because he was sober, there was a question she was dying to ask him. She wondered if she should make small talk or ease into it, but she'd seen him without pants. She figured that afforded her a bit of bluntness. "Tommy, tell me about Task Um."

"Oh, yes, a little side project I started down in Bolivia between pharmacology batches. Originally, it was going to be a Fiverr knock-off, but I decided to do it the other way around. Instead of offering cheap services, people could take spot jobs, like a day-labor agency. It's moderately successful. Even smaller cities have day labor businesses."

"But that's the limit to your involvement? You're not, for instance, arranging criminal conspiracies through it? Murdering people?"

He shook his head. "Of course not." He yawned. Without prompting, he started to talk again. "Well, maybe I manipulated things a few times. It is rather convenient for that sort of thing. I know you were involved in some of the less legitimate tasks."

"So that was you? Why would you want to crash the governor's car?"

"Not that I'd admit to that, but a person might have lots of reasons, I suppose. If they were like me and didn't particularly like government, for one. Or say she was about to help push through some legislation a person didn't like, and removing her involvement meant that a vote would fail and that bill didn't become law. Not that I would do something like that. This is merely speculation. But a shrewd person could turn a few hundred dollars investment into a million-dollar tax break."

"And why would someone murder the assistant Polk County Treasurer?"

"Honest to God, that wasn't me. I think it was a domestic dispute. However, your performance in that scenario impressed me a lot more than your phony resume. The assassin gave you five stars."

"I'm not surprised. He actually offered me a job."

"Really? Well, I'm glad you came to me instead of taking his offer."

"So," Amy asked, "what does this have to do with Satanism?"

"Almost nothing at all, except that all those designer drugs allowed me to see the code of our universe."

"What's that?"

"It's a lot to explain. I'll tell you on the ride home. We've arrived."

This suited Amy just fine, as she now had to explain to a boat load of Satanists why she hadn't bought the movie they wanted, and she was feeling a bit nervous.

After parking the Explorer, Tommy led Amy down a long dock toward a big boat. It had been Debbie's idea to have their meeting on a chartered riverboat, eating hors d'oeuvres and drinking cheap champagne. Amy had to admit, it was an interesting looking boat, with its giant paddle wheel on the back and large smokestacks.

They were greeted by a man wearing a uniform that managed to look a little martial and a little silly at the same time, something between a Civil War soldier and a caterer. "Welcome aboard the riverboat, James Polk. Today we'll be taking a short trip down the Des Moines River. Refreshments are now being served on the top deck."

They walked up a staircase to the upper deck, which was open but covered with a canopy to keep off rain and sun. The others were already there. David Graves sat in a deck chair seemingly relaxed and holding a champagne flute. Dick Storm and Eric Driscoll sat together. Storm seemed sedate enough, but Driscoll looked ready to strangle someone, so nothing had changed there. Debbie stood by the railing looking back at the city and sipping a white wine.

As they reached the top of the stairs, Graves smiled at Amy. "So, you got to meet a Hollywood producer, even if he isn't such a big deal anymore. What was that like?"

"Well..." Amy paused. She could hear her voice shaking. She hated that she couldn't keep it under control. "I'm sorry to report he's about the biggest asshole I've ever had to deal with, present company excluded. He made sure I got a good look at his saggy old balls before we got to the negotiations. And then he refused to let go of *Karma* unless I slept with him."

143

Grinning, Storm said, "So, how much money did you save us?"

Amy felt her cheeks flush. "I didn't. I didn't sleep with him."

Storm's face turned red. "So, we don't have a deal? You should have either talked him into it or taken one for the team."

Debbie held up a hand. "If you're suggesting Amy should have let that creep touch her, forget it. If you wanted to send a prostitute to do your negotiations, you should have thought of that." She sounded pissed that he would even mention it. Amy silently congratulated her stepsister for showing some backbone.

Storm glowered for a moment. "I suppose you have a point," he said grudgingly.

Amy held up her hand. "As a matter of fact, I did talk him into it, I threatened to chop his balls off—"

Graves smiled and held up his cheap champagne in a salute. "Good girl."

Driscoll winced. "Can we not discuss losing testicles, please?"

Graves' smile became decidedly wolfish. "A bit of a sore subject?"

Amy decided to push forward before people started pulling guns. "However, Rich lied to us from the beginning. He sold the film weeks ago."

She gave them a moment to get out their expletives and cleared her throat to get everyone's attention. "Rich refused to deal on *Karma,* yes. However, for a mere two million dollars I was able to pick up *Devil Daze*, the entire trilogy." She stopped and waited to be congratulated.

Storm blurted out, "What?"

Amy continued. "It's just as big a cult classic as *Karma,* plus you can sell streaming rights on all three movies, divide them up or sell them as a set. You'll make just as much money on this deal with less risk."

Storm shook his head. "Do you know what we are, young lady? Do you know who we worship?"

Amy flushed. She thought they'd like a movie associated with Satan. "Well, I'd kind of figured it out—"

"Those films are derogatory. They imply that all Satanists are potheads and pill poppers. I won't be a part of this."

Amy flushed again. She thought she'd done the right thing.

"What do you mean?" Debbie asked. "Are you backing out now?"

"They make worship of the Dark Lord look like a joke, and I won't be a party to their depiction."

Amy felt like things were spinning out of control. "Mr. Storm, I'm sorry. I didn't know you had such strong feelings on the subject."

He shook his finger at her. "My religion is no laughing matter. I happen to take my relationship with the Dark Lord very seriously."

Graves rolled his eyes. "Please, this is a money deal. Do we have to get all emotional? Let's chill out and run the numbers. Besides, those movies are good for recruiting. If people don't take damnation seriously, they've done half our job for us."

Driscoll, perhaps waiting for an opportunity to stand up to Graves, chose this moment to wade into the fray. "Why don't you just shut up, Graves?"

Graves yawned. "Why don't you go fuck yourself?"

Before Amy even had time to blink—not that she would have been willing to stop him—Driscoll shot across the deck like a missile, headed for Graves.

Graves grabbed the empty deck chair sitting beside him and brought it around in a wide arc, crashing it into Driscoll. Driscoll went headfirst over the railing. Amy waited for a splash. Instead, she heard a loud crash. Below, someone screamed. Apparently, Driscoll hadn't been moving fast enough to clear the lower deck.

Storm pulled a gun and pointed it at Graves.

Graves sighed and pulled his gun out in response. "You know, I was really hoping not to repeat this part." Despite how quickly he'd taken action against Driscoll, he sounded bored at the prospect of a gunfight, like he couldn't be bothered.

"You need to stop busting up my people," Storm shot back. "Eric lost a ball when you kicked him."

Amy looked over at Tommy to see if his guns were out. He apparently hadn't even noticed. His eyes were closed, and he was snoring very softly.

As long as everyone else was distracted, Amy availed herself of the hors d'oeuvres and cheap wine. They had little ham and pickle things and some mini cheesecakes. She was sure they came from the Costco freezer section, but she wasn't turning down free even if they were inadequately thawed. Part of her was a little appalled at how blasé she'd become around handguns actually being pointed at people, but none of them were pointed at her. Plus, free food.

Graves smirked. "He seems spry enough now. If you don't want your man hurt, tell him to stop coming at me. Until then, can we put the guns away? Unless you really are going to shoot me, that is."

Debbie smiled, and made a lowering motion with her arms. "I think David had a point. Mr. Driscoll did lose control."

Storm looked mad enough to spit. He stuffed his gun back in his jacket and turned to Debbie. "You need to unload those movies right now. We better not have our names on them by tomorrow."

Debbie didn't seem ready to give up. "I don't think you understand how profitable the streaming rights to these films could be. I did some initial market research. I think we'd recoup our initial investment in fourteen months and make a significant profit in two years' time."

Storm was unswayed. "Abso-fucking-lutely not. If there's one thing we don't need, it's more bad press."

Debbie looked sad. "Well, Amy did go through a lot to get rights to those films. But I suppose I can try to sell them to someone else. We'll probably incur a loss of twenty or thirty percent."

"So, half a million give or take," Graves pointed out. "Are you going to cover that, Storm? This whole movie deal was your idea, and you already stuck us with bribing that stupid bastard from the DOJ."

"I don't have to cover anything." Storm huffed. "I didn't approve the purchase of those movies. Besides, you just killed my right-hand-man."

Graves looked over the railing. "Don't be dramatic. He's moving around. You'll probably want to get him to a hospital, though." He looked over to Amy and Tommy. "How about you, Tommy? Are you going to eat part of the loss?"

Amy nudged Tommy a couple times and said, "I'm afraid he slept through the whole thing. He's been binging on coke and bath salts for three days straight, so he can see between universes or something. Apparently, it's part of his coding process."

The uniformed man who had greeted them before walked up the stairs. "Um, hi, I'm not sure if you noticed, but one of your party has fallen over the railing. He landed on the lower deck, but he's banged up pretty bad. We're turning around so we can meet an ambulance at the docks."

"Thank you," Debbie said.

With business done and everyone mad at each other, all they could do was glower across the deck as the boat returned to dock.

Amy got up and sidled over to Debbie. "So, I guess I royally fucked this up, huh?"

Debbie shrugged. "I doubt I could have done much better. Who would have guessed the old man would be so sensitive?" She paused and said in an airy voice. "Religion makes fools of us all."

"Who said that?" Amy asked.

Debbie pointed to her chest. "I did."

147

"Um, do you know how to offload digital distribution rights?"

Debbie shrugged. "I have no idea, but we figured out how to buy them. We'll figure out how to sell them."

o o o

As the meeting was wrapping up, Tommy shook himself awake, stood up and stretched. "Well, I needed that power nap. What did I miss?" he asked Amy.

"Not much. Everyone pulled guns again, and we had to come back so Driscoll could go to the hospital. Graves threw him over the side."

Tommy shrugged. "How predictable." He pulled his keys from his pocket. "Well, let's say our goodbyes and I'll take you home."

She waited until they were in the car to ask, "So, what about this seeing through universes stuff? How does it tie into Satanism?"

"It doesn't, really. You see, Amy, computers are all about abstraction. Sometimes it's easier if you can look a level up and see how an abstraction layer was written, even do some basic manipulation, if you see what I mean."

Amy shook her head. "Not at all."

"Okay, let's start from first principles. Existence is meaningless."

"But that's got to be wrong. We're literally caught in a struggle between the forces of good and evil."

"So it would seem, yes, but have you ever played a computer game, like a modern, immersive computer game?"

"Sure."

"Everything on the screen can look real, but behind that facade are calculations, graphics files, just ones and zeros strung together in patterns. You turn it off, that world ceases to exist, just like matter, which when you look away compresses into energy waves."

148

"Wait, you're saying we're in a computer game?"

"Think of it this way—an advanced civilization builds a model of itself, to better understand itself. Then that simulation becomes advanced enough and starts building simulations, and so on, and so on, so that there are infinite numbers of civilizations at any given moment, real or simulated, all started from one base civilization—"

Amy nodded. "So, the odds of us being in the base reality are essentially none."

"Exactly."

"But even if there was enough computer power to do something like that, wouldn't we notice things, like weird glitches. Software's not perfect, right?"

"We can't notice because we're programmed not to. We can't recognize the simulation because we are part of it. It's impossible to look outside the limiting factor of the rules of our own universe." He tapped his forehead. "Usually."

Amy was eighty percent sure this was nonsense, but the man's code did work. She had a sneaking suspicion her two black bras had something to do with this as well, but she didn't want to ask and sidetrack the conversation. "But you did that. You broke through the rules or whatever, right? How?"

"I cheated." By the way he said it, she could tell he was very proud of himself. "Like Kirk in the Kobayashi Maru."

"I don't know what that means."

"I started by taking the custom drugs and slowly picking away at my own brain's programming until I found a bug I could exploit—a divide by zero error, coincidentally. Then, I had my way of seeing outside the rules of our universe. It's set up very similarly to an object-oriented database."

"I also don't know what that means."

"I started rewriting little things here and there. The name of a series of children's books. Famous lines from Disney movies, that sort of thing. And it worked.

Most people didn't even notice; they thought their memories were faulty. I even tried some bigger things with some of my Task Um employees—duplicating personal items, changing their address."

"You did that to me," Amy complained.

Tommy nodded. "And you noticed. And I noticed you noticed."

"So, you were spying on me?"

"Spying's a complicated concept when I'm looking at your source code."

Amy sighed. This was all too confusing for straight answers. "So, what does this all mean? If our universe doesn't really exist, how am I supposed to live my life?"

Tommy shrugged. "You don't have to change anything. You're still the same person you ever were, whether you were a soul in a meat sack or a collection of properties stored in a database. Or you could do like me and realize none of your actions have any true meaning, so you might as well do anything you can to make your existence enjoyable. It helps if you want to write literally world-changing code."

"So, I can choose to just forget about everything you just said or become a completely hedonistic sociopathic monster like you."

Tommy nodded. "Technically psychopathic, but now you're getting it."

○ ○ ○

Two hours later, David Graves knocked on Randy Clarke's office door. He knocked softly, not wanting to interrupt Randy if he was meditating. From inside the office, Clarke yelled, "Come in."

David walked into Randy's office. Randy lay on his big leather couch, no doubt waking up from a long nap —he was a big believer in a hands-off management style. "Hey Randy, we've had another setback in the deal."

Randy sat up straight. "How fucked is it?"

David shrugged. "I don't think it's 'fucked' yet, but Storm threw a fit today. We sent Amy to buy a film as a good faith deal. She did the best she could—she's a smart girl—but instead of coming back with *Karma*, the Jason Sizemore film, she came back with *Devil Daze* one through three. Apparently, Rich had already sold *Karma*, and he lured her there hoping for a side deal in his bedroom."

Randy shook his head. "We have to start hiring sleazier lawyers. But what's wrong with *Devil Daze*? I love those films, and I bet they have a bigger following than *Karma*."

"They do. In fact, the lawyer says they'd probably turn a profit sooner and make us more in the long run. But Storm's offended by them. He says they show worshipers in a poor light."

"Of course they do," Randy said. "That's what makes them so fun. I worship the Dark Lord. I don't see a problem with the films."

"Well, he doesn't appreciate the irony as much as you do. He wants to dump the whole deal."

"What does that mean for us?"

"We might have to eat part of the loss, well, all of the loss."

"So, Storm's throwing a shit fit over his precious dignity, but we have to eat any shortfall? We just offered a million-dollar bribe to a fed."

"I know. But I think the risk is worth it. We can cover it. Remember how cash-flush MediaStorm is."

"Oh, sure, we can cover it, but if this deal doesn't pan out, nobody's getting an anti-Christmas bonus this year. And I am personally going to make sure Dick Storm dies soon. *Without* his balls."

"That's a, um... disturbing image." David wondered if he should mention that he'd already taken a testicle from Storm's right-hand man, but he didn't think that would be enough to console Randy.

"Because I'm going to cut them off, you see."

David nodded. "Yeah, I got that the first time." With all the talk of testicle mutilation lately, he made a mental note to invest in an athletic cup.

Randy seemed lost in thought for a moment. "Say, David, as long as Calltelestar is going to take a loss on this sale, and there's a high profit margin for anyone who buys this trilogy, you want to go halves with me? We'll borrow a couple million, start our own media company, and license the movies."

David shrugged. "Sure. If we can get a line of credit that big, I'm in."

○ ○ ○

After Tommy took Amy home, she thought it might be a nice gesture to look in on Eric Driscoll. Yeah, he was kind of obnoxious, but the poor guy had been beaten up pretty badly. She drove to the hospital and found Dick Storm sitting in the waiting room. "Hi. Tommy sent me over to make sure everything was all right with Eric." She sat down across from him.

Storm gave her an appraising look. "No he didn't. That junkie was bombed out of his mind. He didn't have two functional brain cells to help himself. He definitely wasn't thinking about my people." He paused. "Sorry for going off in the meeting. I'm sure you did the best you could. I just get emotional about the Dark Lord."

"Religion makes fools of us all," Amy quoted.

"That's deep. Who said that?"

"Debbie."

He gestured to her. "You're a very shrewd lady. Ever think of joining Team Hades? Would you rather serve in Heaven or rule in Hell?"

"I'm not religious," Amy lied. "I just want to get this merger done, get a cushy job as Tommy's Des Moines office manager, and go back to clubbing five nights a week."

"Come on, you sound like you're on our side already."

"So," she said, "how is Eric doing?"

"Oh, he should be fine. He's going to need a little reconstructive surgery, but nothing like last time. You know, when Graves kicked Eric in the crotch, he ruptured one of his testicles."

Amy nodded. "Yes, you had mentioned."

"Yeah, popped it like a grape. That's what he gets for fucking with someone as powerful as Graves. They can use a silicone implant now, so the sack feels the same."

"So, Graves is a powerful..." She paused, wondering if she should use the word, but Justice said it was a pretty open secret, and Storm had just tried to recruit her. "...Satanist."

"Yeah, a real coup for Calltelestar to get him. They found him by accident, working on the phones. He had an affinity for the dark arts from day one. He's only been practicing for a couple years, but he's a natural. When the merger is done, they'll probably put him in charge of MediaStorm and tuck Eric and his big title somewhere he won't hurt himself."

Amy nodded. "Um, you're being awfully candid for a..."

"A Satanist with his own agenda?" He smiled. "Maybe you just have an honest face. Maybe I'm just an old man who's a sucker for a young girl. Besides, aren't we all just one big happy family?"

"I...uh..." She didn't know whether he meant part of the merger, or including her in the Satanic inner circle, official membership notwithstanding. Personally, she didn't see how someone could know there was a God and choose to worship the Devil.

That started her thinking though, was there a third choice? Could there be people out there worshiping Odin, or Ra, or Pan? Did they make personal appearances? Sure, God hadn't done a face-to-face in a while, but she was sure it was difficult to get a meeting with Jay-Z and Beyonce. Meeting God had to be much, much more difficult. She'd heard some guy had paid five million dollars to have lunch with Warren Buffett.

"You still with me, sweetie?" Dick Storm asked. Usually, she thought men using condescending pet names with women was gross, but when Storm did it, it was somehow worse, like she was being addressed by a sweet old grandfather with a history of sexual assault.

"Sorry, just lost in thought about the whole good and evil thing."

"Yeah, pretty amazing when you think about it. We're going to win, you know."

"What?"

"The war. The whole war between Good and Evil."

"Are you sure about that?" In her experience, they could barely even manage a little corporate merger without killing each other.

He held up his hands for emphasis. "Look at the world around you. You think all this happened by accident?"

Amy had to admit, the guy had a serious point. She started to feel a little sick. She hadn't eaten anything today but a couple appetizers at the meeting, but suddenly, her stomach felt like it was too tight and too full. "But what about the Bible? It says that... the other side will win."

Storm chuckled. "Propaganda. It is, after all, *their* book. Nah, don't worry. We've got this in the bag. What do they have? *Capax Dei*? Some secret group of priest commandos. It's just a bedtime story Satanists tell their children scare them into misbehaving."

The hospital waiting room started to slowly spin. She stood up. "I should go."

Storm stood with her. "Are you okay? You look a little pale."

Amy shook her head. "I just need some fresh air. You know, hospitals." She left it at that, as if it might explain her sudden queasiness. As she walked to her car, Storm's words repeated in her head, *"We're going to win, you know."* Even if the eternal struggle between good and evil was merely part of some advance simulation, she still had to live here.

10

Divine Guidance

In a sedate, beige conference room with large, friendly windows displaying a view of Infinity, Amy appeared. This surprised her, as she clearly remembered going home and going to bed. She also felt a little disconcerted as she only wore a tank-top and panties. Given her apparent teleportation and state of undress, she guessed she was about to get involved in angel business.

If they were going to magically beam her up in the middle of the night, they could at least provided her with a robe. Angels were robe people, weren't they? They were always wearing robes in paintings, at least. Then again, Ottoel wore an old suit, so maybe the robes were an aesthetic choice.

She almost called out for Ottoel, but on the small chance that she had been roped into demon business, she kept her mouth shut, and sat down at the conference table, lowering the chair to somewhat hide her state of undress.

A few minutes later, Ottoel entered with another angel. At least Amy guessed it was an angel. It was either the most beautiful man she had ever seen, or the most masculine-looking, gorgeous woman she had ever seen. Either way, the androgynous angel was wearing a robe. Where Ottoel looked like a chubby father-type character actor, this angel looked like something Michelangelo would have sculpted when he was having a particularly good year.

Sitting, the new angel addressed her. "I am Lucael, Ottoel's supervisor. We've brought you here, holy warrior, for a briefing. Plus, I thought it would be nice if we could meet. Sorry about the sudden relocation, but I haven't been on Earth for a few hundred years, and I didn't have time for a refresher course and updated appearance." He pointed to his face. "Hence the Italian Renaissance look."

"Speaking of appearance," Amy said, "I'm not exactly dressed for a meeting."

Ottoel's eyes opened wide, as if he'd just realized she was in her underwear. "Oh. Sorry." He snapped his fingers, and a robe appeared around her. However, there was something odd about it, a logo. "Was this stolen from a Marriott?"

He shrugged. "They expect you to take them, or so I've heard."

Lucael glowered at them. "Can we get back to business?"

"Before we get into that," Amy said, "I've got to ask you something. Dick Storm told me that we, meaning our side, God and the Angels, are losing the war."

The two angels looked uncomfortable. After a moment, Lucael spoke. "We believe God is playing a long game. Things do look dark now, but remember, we've come a long way. We survived the Dark Ages. We can survive the Information Age. Besides, we have people like you on our side, the Lord's holy warrior."

Amy blushed. "I don't really feel like much of a holy warrior. So far, I've just sat in meetings and read some paperwork. Wait, what was your name again?"

"Lucael."

"Lucael, like Lucifer?"

He shook his head and chuckled. "No, nothing like that. Lucifer means 'child of God, bringer of light.' Lucael means 'child of God coming from a bright place.' It's Fifteenth Century Italian. Totally different."

"And Ottoel?" she asked.

Ottoel blushed. "Wealthy child of God."

In his shabby suit, Ottoel was hardly the poster child for wealth. Maybe angel names were as arbitrary as human names.

Amy nodded. "Okay. And so, I'm supposed to make a difference with this merger?"

"Actually, you've already defied the odds by getting as far as you have. According to our best projections, the merger was going to collapse before the point it has reached."

"And, my goal is to make this merger happen?" Amy asked. "I'm not supposed to stop the evil Satanists from merging into a bigger evil organization?"

Lucael gestured to the negative and said, "Not at all. You're supposed to make it all possible."

"Really?" Amy was surprised at this. "And the odds you talked about. Do you have some kind of oracle to figure that out? Or do you use some kind of advanced statistical analysis?"

Ottoel shook his head. "Actually, we have an office pool."

Amy had to ask. "What do you bet with?"

Ottoel shrugged. "Bragging rights mostly. It's just a way to pass the time. Most of the choir of angels thought that Storm would have shot Graves by now, or vice versa. Of course, that's why we brought you in, to keep things moving smoothly."

"I'm not really sure what I'm supposed to be doing."

"Just make sure the merger goes through," Ottoel said. "Make sure no one is killed."

Amy made a face. "Um, Storm's assistant, Eric. He was alive the last I saw him, but he didn't look very good either."

Lucael turned to Ottoel. "Did you know about this?"

"Um yes." Ottoel produced a folder from seemingly nowhere. He flipped through it. "Eric Driscoll's nose is broken, he's down a testicle, and he is going to need some dental work, but he's otherwise unhurt."

Lacael shrugged. "He's not really that important in the greater scheme. If Driscoll ends up in the basement, the universe will survive."

Amy nodded. "Okay, then." She thought for a minute. "Hey, the merger's actually a little stressed right now, because my sister bought up this trilogy of films called *Devil Daze.* Is there any way that maybe you guys could cover a shortfall of a couple million or so?"

Lucael chuckled and shook his head again. "Why do you think angels would have money?"

"I've seen what Rome looks like. Couldn't the pope write me a check?"

Ottoel shook his head. "That would be a miracle."

"Okay, so miracle me up three million dollars?"

"I thought you needed two million," Ottoel said.

Amy shrugged. "I have expenses."

"Absolutely not," Lucael said. "It's kind of a rule, has something to do with economics. Only the Federal Reserve can just print money for no reason. Besides, how are you going to explain the money to your boss and his partners?"

She nodded. "Okay. Fair point. I still don't know how or why I'm expected to hold together this merger."

Lucael stood. "That is for you to figure out." He turned his back on them and left.

Amy turned to Ottoel. "Any advice on how to save the merger?"

Ottoel looked a little nervous. "Advice, yes. On the merger, not really." He hesitated for a moment, then he said, "You were going to give Holden that sword, right?"

"Yeah." She'd totally planned to, but she hadn't gotten around to that.

"Do it now."

"What? I know we're on a different plane of existence and everything, but didn't you pull me up here in the middle of the night? Won't it still be the middle of the night when you return me?"

"Just trust me," Ottoel said. "The moment I send you back, grab that sword and go over to Holden's place. I shouldn't have told you that much. I'm breaking the rules as it is, but he's been good to you. You need to go return the favor."

"Okay," Amy said, unsure of how to feel about the lack of detail he was giving her. "But I'm taking time to put on some pants and a bra."

"Fine, but hurry." He snapped his fingers.

The beige room winked out of existence, and she was back in bed.

○ ○ ○

Amy crawled out of bed and started searching for something to wear. She threw on a sports bra, t-shirt, and yoga pants. She probably looked like she was going to the gym, but something about Ottoel's insistence made her think speed was probably more important than style. She grabbed the sword and hurried over to Holden's apartment.

She knocked on the door twice before she gave up and called his phone. She heard it ringing through the door, and eventually he picked up. "Amy? Do you know what time it is? I worked a ten-hour shift today."

"I'm outside. I have something for you. Open the door."

"What?" He sounded somewhat annoyed and very sleepy, but after a few seconds, she heard his door unlock. It opened, and he stood squinting at her, wearing just a pair of sweatpants, and showing off an impressive amount of lean muscle. "Why do you have a sword?"

She slid past him into the living room. It was mostly dark, he hadn't turned on the overhead light, and she could just see the outline of his furniture through the light cast from his bedroom down the hall.

Holden closed the door, locked it and turned to her. "Well?"

"It's your souvenir from California, remember?" Thinking better of telling him an angel insisted on the visit, she softened the truth a bit. "I had a dream that you were in danger. I guess it's silly, but I woke up and had an impulse to bring it over."

"The sword used by Kirk Douglas?"

"Douglas Fairbanks. I think he was from the silent movie days."

"Well, um..." Holden said, "Thanks for the sword and all, but I probably should get back to—" He stopped suddenly and turned toward the door. A quiet, clicking sound came from the door knob. He put his finger over his lips, telling Amy to be silent, and gestured to her to step backwards. She backed away until she stood to the side of the door, where she'd be impossible to see by anyone walking inside.

Holden stood to the other side of the door. He looked ready to spring.

The clicking sound continued for a moment, and the door lock slowly rotated. A moment later, the doorknob slowly turned. The door swung open, and someone extended an arm into the room, holding a handgun with a silencer on it, just like in the movies. Holden sidestepped the gun's muzzle, grabbed the arm and pulled.

Off balance, a huge man stumbled into the room. Holden tried to get a better grip, but before he was able, the man punched Holden in the face with his free hand. Holden fell down, and the man aimed his gun.

Amy felt the buzzing sensation inside her head, and without even thinking, she struck out with the sword. The stage prop was relatively dull, but she struck the big man on the wrist, making him drop his gun. He turned to face her, but she hit him again with the sword, this time on the top of the head. It seemed to do the job.

He went, "Oof," and fell to the carpet.

She was afraid she might have killed him, having never knocked a man unconscious before. Amy reached over and turned on the overhead light. She recognized the man, Barney, the assassin she'd given a ride to the vet. "O-M-G!"

Holden sat up and shook his head. "What?"

"I, um..." Amy thought. "I think I might have killed him."

Holden got woozily to his feet and then grabbed the gun gingerly by the barrel. "That guy hits hard. If he moves, yell. If you need to, hit him with the sword again. I'm going to get my cuffs and call this in."

Amy waited, but Barney didn't stir. She took a moment to ponder that if she'd taken the job with him, or even if she'd just stayed with Task.um, she might be on the other side of this encounter.

She wondered if he would recognize her if he woke up. She could be in big trouble if he revealed her as an accessory to murder. She thought about hitting him again with the sword, harder this time, to make sure he was dead. But even as she considered, she knew she couldn't. Besides, he'd have to confess his own role to incriminate her. She was probably safe enough.

Holden came back, wearing a t-shirt and his cop belt over his sweatpants. He took a pair of steel handcuffs out of a pouch, pulled the man's arms behind him, and locked his wrists into them.

Once the man was secure, Holden took out his radio and announced his badge number. When the dispatcher responded, Holden gave them his address and a series of codes, which Amy did not understand. After a minute of talking, Holden reached over and lowered the sword, which Amy had been holding at the ready.

Thirty minutes after Holden called it in, there was a knock at the door, followed by a muffled voice saying, "Holden?" By that time, Barney had recovered, and he sat up with his back against one of Holden's chairs, his hands still cuffed behind him. She had seen the recognition in his eyes when he came to and saw her standing over him, but thankfully, he'd kept his mouth shut.

Amy opened the door to find Holden's coworkers, Mark and Johnathon, outside in uniform. She stepped aside and let them in.

Holden nodded at them without taking his focus off Barney. "Took you guys long enough."

Johnathon looked embarrassed. "We were all the way across town. We were the only ones who took the call. Everyone else was too busy, apparently."

The men shared a silence. Amy wasn't used to seeing Holden upset, but he visually bristled at this news. There seemed to be a lot of tension in his pose.

As Mark and Johnathon tried questioning Barney, Amy pulled Holden aside. "What's the deal with no one answering the call?"

Holden shrugged and said softly, "Sometimes you can make enemies just being the wrong skin color, or loving the wrong kind of people, or being the new guy from out of state. Let's just say I tick a lot of people's boxes."

Over the next hour, the rest of Holden's cop friends showed up, plus a few more. Some started knocking on neighbor's doors and asking questions. Some started searching the parking lot for Barney's car. They put Barney's gun in an evidence bag, but they also took away the sword.

Another twenty minutes passed, and Elliot showed up wearing a suit that had seen better days. The uniformed officers deferred to him, calling him Detective. He had Holden go through everything that had happened.

When Holden got to Amy, he just said, "Amy came over around three. She said she had a bad dream about me, and she was worried. She brought over the prop sword, a souvenir from her California trip, as a gift. She really saved my life."

Amy felt herself blush.

"Is this true?" Elliot said. "Did you really just have a dream and wander over?"

Amy shrugged. "Yeah, I only live a couple buildings away."

"What kind of dream was it?"

While she could remember her meeting with the angels in detail, she didn't really want to share. She made a face and tried to look like she was thinking about it really hard. "I can't really remember. I think it involved a guardian angel and a conference room."

Then the uniformed officers told their versions of the story, including the questioning and the fact that the "suspect" had remained silent the entire time.

Elliot nodded. "You're not going to get him to talk either. The FBI sent over some pictures of likely suspects for the county auditor's office shooting. This guy's name is Emil Poproski. He's Polish mafia, a real hard ass. You're both lucky to be alive."

11

On Exhibit

The next day, Justice Labrador called Amy at work. "I am going to take you to the Iowa State Fair."

"No, you're not."

"I thought you small-town girls were into that sort of thing, showing hogs, 80s hair bands, fried butter, tractor pulls..."

"Sorry, not me. Blame my poor upbringing, but I was more into Barbie."

"Well, yes, when you were little, but what about when you got older, you must have—"

"High stakes online Mah Jong." This was Amy's typical sarcastic response to the question. Besides, why should she feel ashamed that she played with Barbie until it was time to go to college when there were fully-grown men who still played video games? "I got too good, and the Yakuza sent some goons after me, so I had to give it up."

He paused as if digesting this for a second. "I'm not sure if you're being sarcastic. If you don't like the fair, how about a second date at a nice restaurant not owned by David Graves?"

Amy leaned back in her chair and sighed at the phone. While she didn't want to lead Justice on, she wouldn't mind having him as a friend, and she had been rather blunt about her lack of romantic interest, so at this point, she felt that any pursuit on his part was his own fault. "I already told you I don't date." She had given him an opening.

"How about a dinner between friends?"

"I might be talked into that."

"Do I still have to pay?" Justice asked.

"Can we invite Holden along, since it's just friends?" She almost felt bad making the suggestion. Lately, she felt she'd been spending too much time with Holden. He was new in town. She shouldn't be monop- olizing his time. He might be a great wingman, but he should be able to make other friends.

"How about it's just the two of us, we won't call it a date, and I'll pay? I prefer one-on-one conversation. In a three-way, you always have to decide who to pay attention to."

Amy was sure he meant the double entendre. She ignored it. "You sound like you still think you have a chance. Didn't I just mention that I'm not into dating? Or don't you like Holden?"

"I find Holden charming." Justice sounded amused by her suggestion. "In fact, maybe I should ask him out to dinner instead."

"You should. You'd have a better chance of getting laid, especially if you wore a cowboy hat and a denim jacket."

He sighed. "That's a deal-breaker for me. I don't own any denim, and I've never been a hat guy."

Amy wasn't sure whether he really just wanted to hang out or if she was leading him on. She decided to give him the benefit of the doubt. "Do you even know of any restaurants in town not owned by David Graves?" Since her heart-to-heart with Graves, she had to admit, she had softened to him a notch. However, that didn't mean she wanted him showing up while she was trying to eat.

"There's the Gearbox."

"The biker bar? I thought that was a rough place."

"Depends on who you go with. I've represented half those guys in court."

"Point taken. I prefer places where the jukebox isn't blasting Steppenwolf, though."

"What about Dang O'Keeffe's?"

"I've never heard of it."

"You'll love it. The best Vietnamese potato bar in the city."

"That's a thing?"

"It's fusion cuisine."

Inwardly, Amy cringed at another fusion experience, but maybe O'Keefe's would be a little more palatable. "Okay. I'll give it a try."

"Great. Dang's is just down the street from the State Historical Building. Have you ever been there?"

"No. Graves mentioned it the other day, though. Have you?"

"Once or twice. I thought it might be a neat place to visit on a... platonic outing. Let's meet there in an hour, and we will have time to look around before we eat."

He hung up before Amy had a chance to say no, thus making their dinner even more date-like. Still, she found herself looking forward to getting out of the house and going to a place where no one would be assaulted or pull out a gun over the hint of disrespect. One day away from Satanist nonsense was exactly what she needed.

○○○

Amy parked on the street behind the Historical Building, and before she could get out of her car, Justice Labrador parked right behind her.

She got out of the car and waited for him. When he opened his door, she said, "That was perfect timing."

"I was actually behind you on coming off the ramp." He nodded to the large building in front of them. "It's pretty impressive inside, but I guess it's partially under construction right now. They used to have a restaurant on the roof. If that was still open, I would have taken you there. They had delicious pasta dishes."

"But instead, you're going to feed me potatoes covered in peanut sauce?"

He shrugged. "That is an option, if you so desire. I'm a big fan of the *pho* hash brown soup."

"I don't even care, as long as I don't have to hang out with a table full of Satan worshipers."

"Yep, just the two of us, and assorted members of the public," Justice said. "Actually, the local news did a segment on the museum last night. They're over budget on their remodel. Usually, this place is as quiet as... well, as a museum. I hope they aren't horribly busy today."

They walked into the back door of the building, and Amy was immediately blown away by the huge interior. It was four stories tall, with an open floor plan, giving it a dramatically high roof, from which hung two old-timey aircraft. Unfortunately, the architect had decided to put a huge staircase in the middle of the room, which broke up the space and stood out like... like a giant, metal staircase. Also, because of the remodel, it looked like large sections of the building were closed to the public, sealed behind plastic sheets.

The back door put them on the second floor. Amy leaned over the railing to look at the gallery below.

Quite a few people milled about on the ground floor, no doubt due to the news coverage. By the base of the staircase, she saw David Graves looking at an exhibit with his girlfriend. What was her name again? Blackbird? Crow? Death Pigeon? Raven—that was it.

Amy felt dizzy, and her entire body seemed to jolt with adrenaline What the hell was going on? Why couldn't she go anywhere without running into David Graves? She grabbed Justice's hand and dragged him behind a hanging sheet of plastic into one of the areas under construction. She glanced around, and while she saw evidence of construction, tools and things, she didn't see any actual people. "Good, we're alone back here."

He raised an eyebrow. "I thought you didn't want to get romantic. Are you trying to steal a kiss?" The he paused, giving her a serious look. "You're shaking? Are you all right?"

"I do not want to steal a kiss," she growled. "David Graves is down there with his psycho-bitch girlfriend. That's two dates where we ran into David Graves." She glared into his eyes. "Are you manipulating this? Are you purposefully going places where you know Graves will be? Are you two working together?"

Justice held up his hands in a surrender gesture. "Not guilty, Your Honor. Coincidences do happen, you know. Or maybe we're just pawns in the cosmic struggle between good and evil, and... How did that go again?"

Amy glared at him for a second. Then, she grabbed his arm. "Let's get out of here." Instead of leading him through the plastic toward the back door, where Graves might look up and see them, Amy glanced around for a different exit, and still seeing none, plunged deeper into the plastic-shrouded area. They weaved around scaffolds and pallets of materials, looking for a back staircase or another exit, pushing through one plastic sheet after another.

"I think we've gone too deep into this labyrinth," Amy said. "Time to head back."

They had circled back to the spot they had come in. Instead of going through the last sheet of plastic, Justice picked up a hammer covered in a thick layer of construction dust. "Should we fight our way out?" He gave her a silly grin.

"Stop fooling around." She made a face. "Put that down. It's filthy."

He complied and tossed the hammer onto a nearby pallet of cement bags.

"Okay," Amy said, "we're going to have to sneak out the way we came in. We'll make a run for it. This will work, right?" Without waiting for an answer, she grabbed Justice's arm and pulled him through the plastic.

They literally ran into Dick Storm and Eric Driscoll. Amy nearly knocked over the older man. "Dick!" she said in surprise. "Eric! Hello. Um. What brings you two here today?" Eric looked worse than ever.

Storm smiled at her. "Oh good, you got my message. The local news did a segment about the place, so Eric and I decided to invite everyone here for a low-stress outing. There's been so much bad blood about this merger. I thought we should do something fun."

Eric did not look happy about that, but then again, when had he looked happy about anything? The two black eyes, neck brace, and cane didn't seem to do much for his look either.

It occurred to Amy that Debbie had planned the boat ride for exactly that purpose, but she kept her mouth shut. It wouldn't be the first time a man had taken a woman's idea and claimed it as his own.

"Besides," Storm said, "after the merger, I might like a low-stress job, and if the renovation is going as badly as they claim, the governor might be looking for a new director for the facility. She and I are close, you know."

Amy nodded. "Oh, and I should introduce Justice Labrador. He's been doing some legal work for Debbie. He produced those financial statements for the government."

The men shook hands, and of course, there was mention of the commercials and the little people. She was trying to think of a way to change the subject when the elevator doors opened, and Graves walked out with Raven.

"Hi, everybody!" Graves said enthusiastically.

"David!" Storm smiled like Graves hadn't almost killed his second-in-command the last time they met. "I see you brought Ms. Stevens..."

"Raven," Raven interjected.

Storm nodded acquiescence "Of course, my dear."

Driscoll mumbled something under his breath.

Amy was wondering how she should answer when Graves asked, "Did you guys see Tommy downstairs?"

"Tommy's here?" Amy asked. She was getting that queasy feeling again. The room was spinning. She took a few deep breaths. She felt like she was on the edge of a panic attack.

Graves nodded. "I assumed he came with you. He's passed out on one of the benches."

"Amy," Justice asked, "are you okay? You look pale."

"I think I need to..." She took hold of the cold metal railing. After a couple minutes, the rooms stopped spinning, and she looked up to see everyone staring down at her. She felt embarrassed. Everyone was on their best behavior, obviously trying to save the merger, and she was causing all the drama. Flushing with embarrassment, she let Justice and Graves help her straighten up.

"Are you all right, Amy?" Graves asked.

She nodded. "Just a dizzy spell. I think I just need something to eat."

"We were about to go to Dang O'Keefe's," Justice offered.

"Great, then," Storm said. "Let's go get Tommy."

They walked down the grand staircase and found Tommy sleeping on a bench in a hallway next to an exhibit about Iowa's involvement in the Civil War. Amy gave him a nudge.

Tommy opened his eyes and yawned. "What are you all doing in my office?"

"Tommy," Amy said, "You're in the State Historical Building. Do you remember how you got here?"

Tommy blinked. "I just tried a new sample from my chemist in Bolivia. I remember reviewing a section of the Calltelestar code and sitting down to watch the news. After that, it's just a blur." He paused to think for a moment. "I'm hungry. Anyone else hungry?"

Justice glanced at Amy and shrugged apologetically. "How do you feel about Irish-Vietnamese fusion?"

"Is that food?" Tommy turned a shade of green that would have been perfect for a St. Patrick's Day celebration. "Sure. Let's go."

Amy knew the guy was self-destructive, but this seemed to take it to a new level.

○ ○ ○

Dang O'Keeffe's was a short walk away from the historical building. It was one of those restaurants that might or might not have decor. It was really too dark to tell, which, of course, benefited Justice's chin. As they were waiting for a table, Debbie walked into the lobby.

Graves waved to her. "Debbie, I'm glad you could join us."

"Thank you. I got Dick's message too late to join you all at the Historical Building, but Justice sent me a text saying you'd be here. It's been forever since I've had corned beef spring rolls."

The nine of them sat in a large booth. "So," Graves asked, "which of the exhibits did everyone like the most?"

"The Civil War," Dick Storm said, immediately. "You know, my great-great-grandfather was taught dark wizardry by Nathan Bedford Forrest himself, after the Battle of Fort Pillow. My family has a history of military service. I myself spent a lot of time in Iraq during the first Gulf War. For a while, I was running Saddam's television station."

From the way Storm was describing his experiences, Amy was having trouble telling which side of the war he'd been on. Did he mean he'd been running the television station after it was captured, or was he running it *for* Saddam? She wasn't the best student of history, but she was pretty sure Saddam had been the bad guy. She glanced over at Tommy, who literally had a picture of Saddam on his wall, but he didn't seem to be paying attention.

Amy glanced at the back of the menu, which had a list of beverages and the story of Danny O'Keeffe and Bich Thoa Nguyen, who had fallen in love during the Vietnam War and come back to live in Iowa, where Bich learned to combine her Vietnamese cooking skills with the Irish-American ingredients Danny loved. Her recipes were the core of the restaurant started by her son, Dang.

Their waitress approached to take their order. While most of them ordered the *pho* hash brown soup or the corned beef spring rolls, Storm ordered the *cao lau* shepherd's pie, Graves ordered the Vietnamese potato pancakes, Raven ordered the baby clam nachos, and Debbie ordered beer cheese *bahn tom* appetizer for the table. After reading the menu and finding out that the restaurant was not a trendy fusion place but an Iowa oddity, Amy enthusiastically ordered the *pho* hash brown soup.

From across the restaurant, Amy saw Holden's cop friends, Howard and Seth, sitting in a corner booth. They weren't in uniform, so she hadn't noticed them at first. However, they didn't seem to be paying her any attention. She tried to keep an eye on them without too obviously watching.

After a moment, Seth started staring at their table and said something to Howard, who also turned to look. Who would they be interested in? Then she remembered—they were investigating Task.um, and they had traced it back to Tommy.

Amy's entire body felt like it was about to burst. If the two cops started questioning her associates, there was no telling what might happen, but she was pretty sure someone was going to get hurt. Tommy was somehow the linchpin to their merger. Did they have enough power to pull strings and get cops fired? Would they put out a hit on the cops, or would they just kill them right here at the table? Maybe she was a little sensitive about the whole murder thing because she'd just saved Holden from an assassination, but there seemed to be a lot of it going around these days.

She felt her stomach tie itself into a knot as they casually dabbed the corners of their mouths, stood up, and started to walk in her direction. She took just a moment to wonder if, in this synthetic universe, there was a subroutine or God that controlled fate, and if that program or entity hated her.

Amy decided she needed to do something before they confronted Tommy. She stood up, strode across to meet the two police officers. She pulled back and slapped Howard across the face. The middle-aged detective looked shocked. "Amy?" he asked.

"How dare you sleep with me and never call me back," she said just loud enough to be overheard by the entire restaurant "Why don't you go back to your wife, you coward?" She grabbed him by the tie and pulled him forward. "Sorry," she whispered. "Please leave. I'll explain later." She didn't know how she was going to explain, but she'd rather not be doing it in front of her violent colleagues.

Seth whispered to her, "What the heck is going on, Amy?"

176

"Those guys at my table are from Calltelestar and Mediastorm. They have powerful friends." She pretended to punch him in the arm. "Just walk away."

Howard grabbed her upper arm. "Are you sure you're going to be all right?"

She batted his hand away. "Leave me alone!" She slapped him across the face. "Liar!" Then she whispered, "Go. I'll be fine."

Howard staggered back. He still looked a little shocked, but he gave Amy an almost imperceptible nod. He grabbed Seth, and they returned to their table, dropped a couple bills and hurried out the building.

Some of the other restaurant patrons applauded.

Amy turned around to find looks of admiration from the Satanist contingent. When she sat down at the table, Raven patted her on the back. "Good for you. I had you pegged as a girly girl, but you can be a tough bitch."

Her cheeks burning, both from the scrutiny of the Satanists, as well as the stares she knew she was getting from the rest of the restaurant, Amy nodded. "What was I going to do?" she said. "Just let the asshole leer at me after he lied to me about his wife? I swear he's been following me."

Dick Storm spoke up. "Do you want me to..." He made a chopping motion across his throat.

She shook her head. "No! No, I can handle him."

Driscoll nodded. "Respect."

A short, stocky man in a suit came over to their table. "I am the owner, and I'm afraid I'll have to ask you to lea—" His eyes widened. "Mr. Graves. Mr. Storm. I'm sorry. I um..."

David Graves took out his wallet. "I'm sorry for any trouble my associate might have caused." He took out two hundred-dollar bills, folded them, and passed them to the man. "Please accept my apologies, Mr. O'Keeffe."

The man nodded. "Thank you. Is there anything I can get you? On the house, of course."

Graves shook his head. "No. We're fine. I appreciate your concern."

After some light dinner conversation, Debbie cleared her throat and segued into business. At first, Amy wondered if this was okay, with Raven and Justice present, but Raven was obviously in the loop on Satanism, and working on some of the financial details, and Justice was arguably more involved in the deal than Amy.

"It's fortunate you all decided to have lunch today. I have good news, but it has to be moved on quickly," Debbie started. "First of all, I was able to offload *Devil Daze* at a loss of only fifty thousand dollars. Minus my fees, of course." This brought appreciative nods from the assembled Satanists, and a relieved look from Graves. "But I also have a new opportunity to bring to the table. I know this is a little outside the norm, but the potential profits are too good."

Debbie paused for effect and then continued, "Are you familiar with the Japanese software Nodenwa?"

"Very familiar," Graves said. "They make the software we use to manage our call center."

Debbie nodded. "Their software runs thirty percent of worldwide telemarketing operations. I was contacted by Mr. Tanaka, their president. Their parent company, Sugioka Technology, is having a bad fiscal year, and they're quietly looking for a buyer to offload the software. The software is actually making money, but it's lost a little market share, and they need an infusion of cash to bring up their short-term numbers and keep their investors happy. Tanaka thought Calltelestar might be interested."

Driscoll spoke up. "I know that company. They're the one with the evergreen tree in their logo."

Graves nodded. "Yeah, it's a little cedar tree on a hill."

Storm smiled. "I like that logo. It's pretty."

Debbie continued, "They're asking two hundred million."

"Whoa," Graves said, holding up his hands, "I know that's a great price, but Calltelestar doesn't have that kind of money. Maybe once the companies are merged, the new president can make that call."

Debbie did her own gesticulating. "I know you can't make that kind of decision right away. But Tanaka is willing to sign a contract locking in the price as long as we put up ten percent in bribe money. The only catch is he wants cash. He's given us a week to decide."

Graves nodded. "I'll have to talk to our board about this."

Debbie turned to Storm. "Dick, are you in?"

Storm sighed as if lost in thought. After a moment, he said, "So, we get to spread Calltelestar's... proprietary software worldwide in this Nodenwa software, but I have to put up ten million right now?"

Debbie nodded. "Seven point eight million as you're only in for thirty nine percent, but yeah, that's where we are."

Storm thought about it for a minute. "Just think how many people that software will contact. We'd be sacrificing a hundred times more souls to Hell." A grin spread across Storm's face. "Yeah. Fuck it. I'm in."

"Tommy," Debbie said, reminding Amy's boss that he was in the conversation. "That's two point four million from you. Can you cover that?"

Tommy nodded. "I'm not that liquid. I'll have to sell some Bitcoin, but sure. No problem."

Debbie smiled, no doubt imaging the legal fees her company would bring in between the merger and acquisition. "Very well. If Calltelestar decides to go ahead, we'll meet in one week with the cash."

Amy looked around the table, and saw greed reflected back in the eyes of everyone assembled. If they'd been cartoon villains, they would have been wringing their hands and twirling their mustaches. They were about to make a whole lot of money, or kill each other trying.

○ ○ ○

"So," Amy asked as Justice walked her back to her car, "now that you've seen the whole crew in action, what do you think?"

Justice considered for a moment while Amy unlocked her door. "You know, they're a lot more intense than I thought they'd be. They didn't even blink when you beat up that guy. And I'm pretty sure Driscoll wants to murder David Graves."

Amy rolled her eyes. "I didn't 'beat up a guy.' Well, not really. He's a cop friend of Holden's. I didn't want him to cause a scene in front of the Satanists. They seem to have a lot of power in this town. I don't want one of Holden's allies to get fired because he pissed off the wrong person. That's assuming they didn't just decide to make him disappear."

"Awkward."

"And then some. Thankfully, he played it cool. I don't really know him that well."

"Well, now you know he also eats at O'Keeffe's."

"I have a feeling that the next time I see Howard, I'm going to have to apologize profusely and probably buy him a few drinks even if I did just save him."

Amy's phone rang. "Speak of the Devil."

"The cop friend?" Justice guessed. Amy wasn't sure if he meant Howard or Holden. At the moment she wasn't sure she wanted to talk to either, but his guess was wrong, nonetheless.

She answered the call and tried to sound happy. "David, what can I do for you?"

"Meet me outside your apartment in thirty minutes."

Before she could say, "No, it's late, and I don't want to do that," he'd hung up.

"Well, I've been summoned by the great and powerful Graves."

"Have fun."

"Yeah, promise that if I don't come back, you'll report my disappearance to the authorities."

"The one you just beat up?"

She gave him an epic eye roll.

Justice smiled. "Don't worry. You've got this. You handled those guys like pros today."

He held out his hand. "Parting handshake?"

Amy sighed. "Well, I'm really not in the mood, but you did buy dinner."

12

Side Deals

Amy had just enough time to go up to her apartment and freshen up. Now, she waited outside for Graves. In some ways, this reminded her of the first night with Tommy, getting into a dangerous man's vehicle with no stated destination. She probably would have told Graves to go fuck himself if he hadn't bared his soul to her and saved her from sexual assault at the hands of a moron.

Graves drove up in a new Lexus SUV. Unlike Tommy, his suit was carefully tailored to accentuate his large physique. He stopped in front of her, leaving the motor running, and motioned for her. She opened the door and jumped into the passenger seat.

Proximity to the man brought Amy's thoughts about him to the forefront. She had known him as the firer of the innocent and blunt object murderer. Then she had known him as the man trapped in a contract who had come to her rescue. Despite having loathed him for so long, she now found him kind of attractive, which just confused her. She wasn't some girl who got crushes on guys just because they looked good in a suit. Justice looked good in a suit, if you didn't get lost in his chin, and she was one hundred percent immune to his charms.

She tried to detach herself from the feelings of attraction and look at him from a distance. He did have brooding good looks, but he didn't seem attractive enough to shock her libido out of its early retirement. He seemed to have some kind of aura around him though, like how movie stars looked just a little more perfect than regular people. That aura of attraction made her want to know how Graves looked under that suit, despite her not wanting to know.

She decided to just ask. "David, why do I find you attractive? I don't even like men."

"I thought you were dating that guy with the ass on his face."

"Justice? He's just a friend."

Then came the questions. "So, you like women?"

"No."

"Kitchen appliances?"

"What? No. I used to date guys, but I realized I was just doing it because that's what people expected me to do. Right now, I'm not really interested in sex or romance. Or at least I thought I wasn't, but I feel strangely drawn to you."

David nodded. "Oh, yeah. As Satanists, we get gifts from the Dark Lord. It's not all just chanting in basements. I got the charismatic and strong package. People find themselves automatically attracted to me, and I can lift a V8 engine out of a pickup truck. That's not an exaggeration, you know. Raven owns a garage and one day her engine hoist broke. I had to go help her." He blushed. "Okay, I did exaggerate. It was a V6."

That explained how he had so easily destroyed Nelson's underwear. "Well, if you have to lose your soul, at least there are a few perks."

"I think it also makes me prone to emotional outbursts, like a supernatural 'roid rage."

Amy thought about David's many physical altercations. "I hadn't really noticed," she lied.

They pulled off the road onto a long driveway. She could see a huge house in the distance, and she wondered if it was a good time to ask what they were doing. She figured she might as well go for it. He hadn't freaked when she'd told him about her attraction. "So, David, why am I here? I probably should know what I'm walking into. I mean, you're not going to try to steal my soul, are you?"

He shook his head. "Of course not. You know what we are. It would be pretty hard to trick you now. I need you to explain this deal to the board president of my company, Charlie Stevens."

"Isn't he, like, your girlfriend's father?"

"Well, yeah, but he doesn't trust anyone."

"Then why would he trust me?"

"People just seem to like you, Amy."

"What about your supernatural charisma?" she asked.

"Oh, that doesn't work on Charlie. He knows me too well, and he's got his own powers."

Dick Storm had also called her likable, which made her think that threatening old men with swords wasn't her only ability. Maybe she had some supernatural charisma of her own.

As they pulled up the long drive, Amy got a better view of Charlie Stevens' house. It wasn't a wannabe hotel like Spencer Rich had lived in, but it would make a great Gothic mansion in a movie. "So, your fiancée grew up in this house?"

"Yeah. You should see her room some time. It's frightening."

"I can only imagine."

He shook his head. "No, you can't. It's pink and frilly, and there are Will Smith posters everywhere."

"Actor-slash-rapper Will Smith?"

"That's the guy."

○ ○ ○

On the inside, the house was surprisingly tasteful, yet still oozing an impression of wealth. The BBC could have shot a period drama in the foyer. A butler took them to Stevens' office; the room would have made a comfortable lair for any mafia don or master of industry.

Stevens sat behind a sizable desk. For one of the Satanic leaders for the area, he looked surprisingly like a sweet grandfather. "Please, Ms. Love, take a seat."

Amy sat in one of Stevens' overstuffed chairs and felt like she would melt into the soft leather.

Stevens paused a beat and then got straight to the point. "My future son-in-law here tells me that I should put up ten million dollars in bribe money to buy a computer software company. As far as I know, all he's good at is telemarketing, bashing people's heads in, and not knocking up my daughter, so I decided I needed a second opinion."

Amy nodded. "Okay, but I don't know how much I can help."

"Can you explain to me, because my idiot future son-in-law can't, how this all got so complicated? We were merging the companies, which I understood, and I thought we all wanted to happen. Then we were sending people to Hollywood to buy movies off a date rapist. And now we're buying software from the Japanese. What happened?"

"Well..." Amy tried to sort out the ideas in her own head. A lot had happened in the last couple meetings. "Storm seems to have cold feet for some reason. He was all in when this thing started, but then he seemed to change his mind. I don't think it was anything David did. I think Storm just had second thoughts." She diplomatically skipped over the protégé with the missing testicle.

"I suppose that's reasonable. Those things can happen." He shrugged. "So, explain the software thing. I'm not much of a computer guy, but you're a millennial—"

Amy tried not to roll her eyes at that. She was Gen Z, but old people always seemed to make that mistake. Her father even did it.

"...so you were born practically connected to the Internet. And David tells me you're smart, so tell me why I should put up my millions for software. I didn't think anyone paid for software."

"Well..." Amy knew very little about computers as well, but she did know a bit about intellectual property law. Plus, she'd sat in all the meetings and paid attention, and she was willing to bluff. "Companies do buy software from other companies. And you aren't just buying the software. You're buying the company that makes it and the ability to change it. You can put your soul-sucking software inside the system, and you'll be sacrificing ten times the souls."

After pondering this for a moment, Charlie said, "Yeah, but there has to be risks to that."

Amy nodded. "Of course. There are always risks, and you're putting up a lot of money." She tried to think up every scenario she could imagine. "Storm or your Japanese co-conspirator could get greedy and try to steal your money. The Sugioka board of directors could figure out the scheme and fire your guy before he can get the deal through. You might get an honest fed who won't take a bribe. Plus, once you start sending your soul-stealing software out to other companies, there's a much larger chance someone will find out what you're doing. Especially if Tommy can't find that bug that occasionally kills people. Even if you get the company bought and start selling your tech, it has to make enough money to stay afloat and not take you down with it. Sure, they've managed to make it look profitable for the sale, but that doesn't mean Sugioka isn't hiding something. If it was doing great, they wouldn't be trying to sell it in the first place."

Charlie sighed and rubbed his chin. "You've given me some very good points to consider." He nodded to Graves. "Keep your cell phone on. I'm going to think about this and give you a decision tonight.

As they were turning out of the driveway, Graves said, "Why'd you do that?"

"Do what?" Amy asked, genuinely confused.

"I wanted you to talk up the deal. You practically told him to cut bait and run. He'd have to be nuts to put up ten million dollars now."

"He's a smart guy. I knew I couldn't dazzle him with bullshit, so I just laid out the risks as I saw them. He knows how big the rewards can be. He needed the full picture so he could manage his fear and greed."

"Manage his fear and greed? What the fuck are you talking about? You just fucked everything up." He pulled the car over to the side of the road, got out, and kicked a NO PASSING sign. He kicked it twice more, and then he pulled the entire post straight out of the ground and threw it like a javelin deep into a corn field. When he was done, he sat down at the side of the road and stared off into the distance.

Amy tentatively got out of the Lexus, walked over to David. "Everything isn't fucked up. Just calm down for a minute. Take a deep breath."

To her surprise, he did.

She sat down beside him. "You doing okay?"

He nodded. "Yeah. I'm doing good. Look, I know you work for Tommy, and for you this is just a work thing, but for me, this is my life. I know I've mentioned before that I don't like being a Satanist. I was tricked into signing my soul away. I don't want to spend eternity in Hell. I just want to live a normal life, maybe have a family."

"But what about Raven?"

"I used to think Raven was the one for me, but people change and grow apart. Plus, there's this prophecy, the whole 'our first born will be the anti-Christ' thing has kind of soured the relationship as far as I'm concerned. I used to think I could make it work, we could stay together and just not do the kids thing, but lately, well, things have been less than ideal."

"Shit," Amy said,

"I don't know, maybe in another life we could have had something. But it's never just her. I'm stuck with her family, and I'm stuck with Calltelestar. Sometimes, you have to move on, you know. I thought I was close. I have a plan, but I need this deal to go through."

Amy nodded, though she probably wasn't the one to give relationship advice. "So, how do you get away?"

"I've spent years trying to look like I'm enjoying the life, doing bad things, playing by their rules. They trust me now. I just need two things. The first is the contract they tricked me into signing to save my soul, and the second is the computer backup of the same. Both are in the safe in the basement, along with four million in cash, money they'll need me to pull in order to do this deal. That was my grand plan. Get their trust, so they would give me access to that safe, to steal back my soul and their computer backup. I knew it was a long shot, but for some reason, it seemed to be working out."

"Well," Amy said, "they do say the simplest plans are the best. And you never know, he might decide to go for it."

David yawned. "Maybe so. Let me get you home." He stood up and offered to help her. As he pulled her to her feet, his phone rang. "Yes, Charlie? Yes, Charlie. Yes, Charlie." He hung up. When he'd put his phone away, he gave Amy a hug. "Charlie's going to go through with it. Tomorrow, the bank is going to send over a couple bank guards with six million, and I'm supposed to get the other four out of the safe. He's texting me the combination."

Amy was pretty sure text messaging was no way to handle security on a safe which held four million dollars and the souls of your minions, but hey, it wasn't her business. "Congratulations. It looks like things are coming together for you."

He nodded, but his expression darkened. "I'm not home and dry yet, though. A lot of things have to go right between now and then."

○ ○ ○

Charlie Stevens hung up the phone and looked across his desk to his visitor. All the time he had worshiped Satan, meeting demons and even conceiving a child with a succubus, he'd never imagined that he would meet an angel, even if from one of the lesser choirs. "So, you think you can pull this off?"

Lucael nodded. "I'll fly in while they're doing the deal, kill everyone and take the money. Earning you a tidy return on your investment. And I'll have a ticket downstairs as the newest fallen angel, with the murder of a holy warrior promised to God already on my scorecard."

"Just make sure you get David Graves too. I'm sick of that guy, barely being evil and not knocking up my daughter after everything I've done for him. Speaking of which, once you're a demon, how would you feel about impregnating my daughter with the anti-Christ?"

Lucael nodded. "That's awesome. I've always wanted to have sex with a human woman, but I never got a chance. I was on the wrong side of the first war."

"She's only half-human, though. Her mother's a succubus."

"All the better. I bet she's smoking hot."

Charlie nodded. "If she weren't my daughter, I'd date her."

Lucael made a face and held up his hands. "Hey now, let's not be gross about it."

○ ○ ○

Amy walked into Paddy's that night intending to apologize to Howard. She spotted the usual guys all sitting around the table, and as she approached, she saw Howard had a black eye.

"Oh, shit. Howard, did I do that?"

"It's not your fault, Amy," Holden told her.

"I got this on patrol today. A fifteen-year-old kid yelled 'all cops are bastards' and cold-cocked me right in the eye. He was shoplifting porno mags. I wasn't even going to take him in. I was just going to make him put them back. And magazines? Hasn't the little shit heard of the Internet?" Howard shook his head. "You know, I've been on the force longer than that kid's been alive. I get so tired of this job."

Seth patted Howard on the back. "You and me both."

Amy did her best to look sympathetic. She couldn't even fathom the idea of holding a job for more than a few weeks. After a commiserating moment of silence, she had to ask, "Have you guys found out anything about the guy who tried to kill Holden?"

Elliot shrugged his broad shoulders. "I've got no evidence, just a working theory. I think it's something to do with that rose bed full of bodies. The local news screwed up and reported Holden was running the investigation. That's the only high-profile case he's been involved in. The hit man, Poproski, is wanted for murder in Poland, so we're probably going to send him back there, but that's for the courts and State Department to decide."

Just then, a waitress came around. Amy held out her credit card. "Another round of the same, and I'll have a rum and Diet Coke."

There was a general muttering of thanks from the police officers. Amy replied with, "Thank Seth and Howard. They saved my butt in the restaurant. I didn't want anyone at my table knowing I hang out with cops or vice versa."

Howard chuckled. "You're right there. We might have been in just as much trouble as you would have been. I don't care for the power those jerks hold, but I can't do much about it."

Amy nodded. "You think you're okay. No one recognized you?"

Howard shrugged. "We're beat cops, no one was going to recognize us in civilian clothes, and while Des Moines can sometimes seem small, I'm pretty sure no one at Dang's knew me anyway, especially at your table."

Seth gave Amy an assessing look. "About that, Amy. What are you doing hanging out with the city's leading Satanists?"

"Can we just say that I have a very good reason and leave it at that?"

Holden added, "She's been hiding something from me as well."

Seth's gaze intensified. "Why don't you come clean with us? It might make you feel better to get things off your chest. Maybe we can help."

Amy thought about what she could tell them. "I can't tell you anything. You'll think I'm nuts."

Holden gave her a sympathetic look. "Try us. We hear crazy things every day. At the very least, we've perfected our poker faces."

Amy opened her mouth and words came flowing out. "An angel of the Lord named Ottoel told me God wanted me to take a job with Tommy Norman. Now

I'm mixed up with all these Satanists doing evil shit, and every time we meet, I think they're going to kill each other and I'm going to be collateral damage."

After a moment of silence, Seth said, "Amy, it's okay if you don't want to tell us. But you should seriously think about it. We're your friends. We can help."

She shook her head. "No. Sorry. I should have known better. I'm talking crazy, of course."

"I don't think you're crazy," Holden said. "You've been acting weird ever since you started working for Tommy Norman. Admittedly, I haven't known you that long, but after that day, you stopped obsessing about what your father would think. And you stopped drinking as much. I mean, you're no teetotaler now, but you're not keeping up with me." He pointed to her sipped-on rum and Diet Coke. "You used to put away two of those for every one of mine."

"Um, yeah." Her face flushed. "The angel healed my liver. I guess I'm healthier now, but it doesn't process alcohol as easily as it used to. I can get buzzed for half the price, so that's not all that bad."

Mark crossed his arms. "I think you're all crazy, believing in good and evil. Believing those nuts over at Calltelestar really have a hotline to the Devil. Do you have any proof?"

Amy shrugged. "I've got nothing. I didn't believe in this stuff either, but David Graves and Dick Storm believe in it. There's a big meeting coming up with a lot of money involved, which is guaranteed to bring out their darker sides. They've wanted to shoot each other since they met, and I think this is going to put them over the edge."

There was a moment of silence around the table. Then Holden asked, "So, what do you plan to do?"

Amy thought about this for a moment. She'd always had a plan. She just hadn't vocalized it. "I'm going to keep my head down, try to look harmless, and hope no random bullets enter my body."

Holden whistled. Then he seemed to make up his mind about something. "I'll come with you. I'll be your bodyguard."

Amy shook her head. "No way. Menial employees don't bring bodyguards, and I can't bring a friend to an illegal deal."

He nodded. "Fair enough, but I think my bullet-proof vest will fit you. I'll lend it to you. It could save your life."

"Sure," she said. "I'd appreciate it."

o o o

Tommy looked through his recent contacts and called one he had not dialed in a few weeks. When the line picked up, he spoke first. "Hi, Marco. This is Tommy. How are things in Bolivia?"

He listened for a few minutes as the gang leader ran down a list of bribes he had paid on Tommy's behalf. "It sounds like business is good. I was wondering, I have a deal early next week, and I could use a few guys as backup."

Marco thought for a minute. "I might be able to get you guys, I have a coyote who owes me some favors. Can you arm them once they get there? If they get caught hauling weapons into the country, someone might take an interest."

"Of course. I'm in America. They sell AR-15s on every street corner."

"So, *Jefe*, where exactly in *los Estados Unidos* are you?"

"Iowa."

"The potato place?"

"No, the other one, with the pigs and the corn."

"I'm going to have to pay them extra. It would be easy to get guys to go to Hollywood or maybe Miami Beach, but no one wants a vacation in the land of pigs and corn. They don't even have Major League Baseball, do they?"

194

"I could throw in some Hamilton tickets. The road show is coming through next week."

"They might go for that."

"I hear it's just as good as the original cast."

Marco guffawed. "Please, *Jefe*, don't lie to me."

"Fine, just do whatever it takes, Marco. There are some bad *hombres* up here. I don't know why, but I've got a feeling that if I'm not careful I'm going to get my head blown off."

"I'll send some of my best men."

○ ○ ○

Amy only had the one drink that night at Paddy's. She got home at a decent hour and set her alarm. They would meet at noon to make the deal—dramatic enough, right? She was just settling into her bed when her phone rang.

"Hi, Amy. It's Mark. I hope you don't mind. I got your number from Holden."

She blinked a couple times and willed herself up from the well of sleep. "No. That's cool. What's up?"

"I wanted to apologize for what I said earlier, about you being crazy. I didn't want to make a big deal of it in front of the guys, but I guess I'm still a little jaded from my upbringing. You see, I was raised Roman Catholic, and my brother decided to be a priest while I decided to be an atheist. He's not just some ordinary priest either. He works for *Capax Dei*. Ever heard of it?"

"Yeah. Storm mentioned it once. Some kind of commando priests?"

"Yeah, that's it. I guess I've been giving my brother so much crap for joining the priesthood, by admitting there might be anything to your story, I'd be admitting I was wrong and he was right."

"Oh, that's okay. I didn't expect anyone to believe it. That's why I hadn't mentioned it earlier. I just thought I better tell you guys what I was into if I turned up dead tomorrow."

"Yeah, and it doesn't matter what I think. It's all about what you and they believe. I just wanted to say I'm sorry."

"Yeah, Mark, no problem."

○ ○ ○

Dick Storm lay in his four-poster bed, crimson silk sheets caressing his naked skin. He reached out and stroked the side of Eric's face. In the days since the boat incident, the bruising had gotten much worse, as the doctors had warned them.

Eric rolled away from him. "Don't look at me. I'm hideous." The man showed the world nothing but aggression, it was only here, with Dick, that he let down his guard and showed his tenderness, his fears and anxieties.

"Eric, you're the person I chose to spend the rest of my life with. Bruises will fade, your nose will heal, but I'll always be in love with your black, empty soul. From the moment I saw you, I knew I had to have you. I killed my wife so I could be with you."

"Yes, I know. But she was really old. I'm sure you would have done that eventually anyway."

Dick nodded. "Okay, you have a point there, I was looking to trade up to a younger model. But I could have used my powers to seduce anyone. I chose you. What do I have to do to prove that I love you?"

Eric looked him in the eye. "Will you kill David Graves for me?"

Dick exhaled sharply. "You ask a lot, my love. That might mess up our Calltelestar deal."

"You see? You care more about your deal than you care about me." He turned away again.

"No. Eric. Look at me. I will kill David Graves and whoever else you want. This is my gift to you."

Eric turned back and they kissed.

196

13

Dealing Damage

Amy lounged in a sweatsuit, watching Holden look through her wardrobe. He turned back to her and shook his head. "I'm afraid you're going to have to wear one of the skirt-suits."

Amy scrunched up her face. "I hate skirt-suits. The only reason I have so many is my father keeps buying them because he doesn't like women to wear pants, especially in church." She'd always wondered why he kept dragging her to church so often, since he didn't seem to be that into it. Probably a concession to her "holy warrior" upbringing.

"I know." Holden nodded. "You've told me." A moment later, he added, "At great length."

"Okay." Amy took a swig of her rum and Diet Coke. "Pick one out for me. Not the green one, though. I don't want to look like Junior Miss Leprechaun."

"How about this navy blue one? It has nice square shoulders on it. It will help hide the line of the vest."

Amy nodded. "Great. I can look like I play football as a side gig."

"Better a linebacker than dead. We're going for inconspicuously bulletproof, not sexy."

"Point taken." She took another gulp of her drink.

"And take it easy on those."

She raised an eyebrow. "You don't seriously expect me to handle today sober, do you?"

"No, but you have to be sober enough to drive yourself to the office to meet up with Tommy. It would be a shame if I went through all this trouble to keep you alive, just to have you get in a car accident."

"You're right. I'll put this in a sippy cup and finish it in the car once I get there."

"If you do get shot, alcohol prevents clotting."

"You seem to know a lot about getting shot."

He nodded. "I am a trained first responder, you know."

Amy sighed. "Fine. I'll just go get a soda." She wandered into the kitchen and looked through her cupboard. She grabbed a plastic water bottle and poured her drink into it. Then she topped it off with more of each of the key ingredients, namely rum and Diet Coke. Holden didn't need to know.

When she returned, Holden had set out her clothes. He began a lecture as she changed. "Now what do we do if people start shooting?"

"Hide behind something large, preferably metal. If I think I can safely run, do so, but not in a straight line, and always try to put something between me and anyone with a gun."

He nodded. "Good, and then?"

"Call nine-one-one. I can try to call down my guardian angel, but nine-one-one first, because God moves in mysterious ways, but police officers respond quickly and follow procedures." She neglected to mention how many officers had failed to show up when someone tried to kill Holden.

Amy slipped out of her sweats and started getting dressed. Holden politely looked the other way despite, or perhaps because of, his disinterest in her gender. "I'd still rather be there with you."

"That's a big no. These guys act like crime bosses. If they caught a hint that you might have police training, that might be what starts the shooting."

"I'll abide by your wishes." Holden frowned. "I don't have to like it though."

Amy shrugged. "That's the way it is. Besides, I'm a holy warrior. I probably have some kind of divine protection. Maybe I should have a sword. Do you think we could find a sword on short notice?"

Holden pulled his vest over her slip. "You're lucky I'm small for a cop. This vest size is a special order." He started tightening straps. "Have you ever considered, Holy Warrior, that the divine help you've been sent is a cop who is small enough to share his bullet proof vest?"

○ ○ ○

Ottoel stood at the foot of the stage in the Des Moines Civic Center, the neutral ground chosen for the meeting. He scanned the huge room, looking for a hiding place to watch the proceedings. Of course, he could make himself invisible, but with Satanists involved, there was always the chance of a demon strong enough to see through his invisibility. Plus, he wouldn't have to worry about bumping into someone.

Lucael appeared next to him. "Hey, how's it going?" He was wearing a long coat—obviously he hadn't realized it was too warm for heavy outerwear. Ottoel would have to advise him of this later.

199

"I thought you weren't going to come down because of the whole face thing."

"I changed my mind." Lucael stretched. "Besides, I'm not going to be walking around, showing this face to just anyone. Have you done a security sweep of the roof?"

"Do you think we need to?" Ottoel asked.

"Let's just pop up there and have a look to be safe."

Ottoel concentrated for a moment and shifted to the roof. The top of the Civic Center was a flat tar and gravel job, easy to walk on. Ottoel turned around in a circle and saw nothing out of order.

A moment later, Lucael appeared beside him. After a quick look around, he said, "I guess everything looks good up here." He paused. "Ottoel, have you had basic combat training?"

"Of course, before the first time I came to earth. That seems like a million years ago." He thought for a second. "Actually, that may have been a million years ago."

Lucael nodded. "Did they have you fight against a demon sword?"

He shook his head. "No. Do they do that now?"

"Not usually, but let me show you something." Lacael drew a short sword with glowing red runes down the blade. "I got this out of the armory. Look at this inscription."

Ottoel made a face. "How can you even hold that thing? I can feel the evil radiating off— Ow!" Ottoel felt a sharp pain and looked down. The sword was now stuck deep into his body.

o o o

Lucael took cover behind an air conditioning unit as Ottoel's body exploded into a pillar of fire. He waited for the radiated heat to subside and walked around the unit to retrieve his sword. It still glowed red hot from the angelic explosion. All the gravel on the roof as well as anything facing Ottoel had been blackened with soot. The angel's body was completely gone.

Lucael's vision blurred for a second, and he felt a tugging at his cheekbones. He popped down to the Civic Center's men's room. His skin had taken on a green palor, and little spikes now protruded from his face. Damned annoying how doing evil had such immediate corrupting effects.

And then all the feathers fell out of his wings.

○ ○ ○

In the Calltelestar building's basement, David opened the safe and set a duffel bag in front of it. To his left, Randy Clarke looked over his shoulder. To his right stood Julie, their HR demon.

About a year ago, Julie had gone to Hell and gotten a new body. Her old body had been declining quickly from years of doing evil. After the change, she changed her identity and started going by Julia, but David knew her well. She'd sexually harassed him until he'd finally had to fight her off with a hammer and hit her over the head with a computer. Since then, she'd cooled on him, telling him, "A girl can take a hint." David hadn't bothered to point out that she could not, in fact, take a hint, which is why he had to use the hammer. She'd started to go a bit green again, meaning she was burning quickly through her new body.

David carefully stacked $5,000 bundles of cash into the duffel bag. This bag would carry less than four of the 9.8 million dollars. The rest was waiting upstairs between two armed guards. Once they returned from the basement, the money would be packed into David's company car, and he would drive it to the meeting site.

Halfway into stacking the money, David shifted his weight and pushed on his pants pocket. Inside that pocket was a little remote control.

Julie's head snapped up. "Do you hear that?"

201

David tried not to show any emotion as the demon stood up and wandered away. "There's some kind of noise coming from over here."

With Julie walking away, Randy Clarke couldn't help but turn to watch her. In that second, David reached over, and instead of grabbing a stack of cash, he grabbed a stack of documents and a computer back-up tape.

Clarke continued to wander away. "Julie? What are you doing?"

David quickly scooped up another handful of cash and used it to cover both the documents and the tape. When he finished this, he pressed the button on the remote control again.

"It stopped." Julie said. She turned and walked back.

"What stopped?" David asked.

"It was like a high-pitched electronic noise." She turned her head like she was still trying to listen for it. "You probably couldn't even hear it with human ears."

Randy shrugged. "No, I didn't hear a thing."

David had gone to PetCo two days ago and bought the L'il Scrappers Bark Suppression collar as soon as he knew the plan, and who would be looking over his shoulder. The L'il Scrapper used ultrasonic waves to annoy dogs and stop them from barking, so he'd assumed it would also work for demons. He knew it wasn't the most intellectual plan, but it was all he could think of. Distract Julie, who would distract Randy—it wasn't hard to distract Randy. Yesterday, he'd snuck down to the basement and hid the collar in one of the wall vents.

He was kind of amazed it had worked.

○ ○ ○

Tommy parked his Ford by the rear entrance of the Civic Center. Amy looked at the other vehicles parked there. She recognized Debbie's car, and the

Lexus SUV was one of Calltelestar's company vehicles, which meant the Jaguar must have been Dick Storm's.

She turned to her boss. "Tommy, I have a bad feeling about this."

He shrugged. "Don't worry about it. I am a survivor." They got out of the SUV, and Tommy went around the back to pull out a super-sized Aldi bag loaded with two million dollars.

Amy had to comment. "I didn't know Aldi had bags that big."

"They're not by the register, you have to go around the corner," Tommy said. "I was going to have a South American death squad here to protect us, but they were caught at the border."

Amy wasn't sure if he was joking or not.

"Which reminds me, have you seen *Hamilton*? I have some tickets I won't be using."

They tried a back door next to a huge loading dock. It was open.

When Debbie called Amy with the site of their meeting, Amy had asked why she had chosen the Civic Center as their neutral ground. Debbie had been thinking of the place because she had tickets to the *Hamilton* show next week. She'd bribed one of the custodians to leave the back door open, or rather she'd paid Justice to bribe the custodian—just another day in the life of a perfectly reputable lawyer.

They entered into a huge backstage area. Debbie had texted instructions on how to find their way through the building. They took a right into the green room, exited to the lobby, and went through the main doors. Debbie, David, Dick, and Eric waited in front of the stage.

Debbie waved as they walked through the rows of chairs to meet everyone.

"You're late," Graves said. "Why the holdup?"

Tommy had picked Amy up around twenty minutes later than she'd expected. She looked to him, and he answered, "When you've looked beyond the veil of real-

203

ity as far as I have, a few little numbers on a clock seem inconsequential."

"Well," Storm said with a smirk, "I'm glad you were able to see through this inconsequential reality long enough to join in our little venture. I hope all the little numbers on your money are correct."

Debbie cleared her throat and put on her serious voice. "Good afternoon, gentlemen, Amy. I can't wait to tell you what I just found out." She paused for effect. "Today, Strategic Partnerships, LLC, Nodenwa's primary competitor in call center management technology, announced the end of life cycle to their Call Sweet Suite. They will not be coming out with a new version."

Storm raised an eyebrow. "Do you mind putting that into plain English for the rest of us?"

Debbie brought out her smug voice. "It might take a few years, but Nodenwa is going to rise significantly in value, as well as market share. And as long as we pool this money and deliver it to Japan by Sunday, we have a locked-in price. I've taken the liberty of chartering a jet. I can be in Kyoto tomorrow. If any of you have your passports in order, I propose we go together. We can have a mini-vacation and celebration, visit the old capitol, drink some *sake*, and be back home in time to rest up for Monday. Consider it a bonding exercise. After all, as officers of the new company, you will be spending a lot of time together."

Amy watched the assembled men. David and Dick looked conflicted. Eric looked pissed off as usual. Only Tommy seemed happy at the prospect of a mini-vacation in Japan. A moment ago, she feared for her life, standing around with dangerous men and stacks of money, but now there was a possibility of even more money. Were they really going to pass up the chance to get even richer in exchange for a gunfight? She even started to wonder if her passport was up to date.

Everyone seemed to be nodding in agreement, except for Eric. Storm turned to him, "Eric, this sounds like a good deal. Maybe—"

Whatever Storm had been about to say was lost as Eric let out an animalistic scream. Amy wasn't startled or alarmed as he pulled out his gun. She'd seen so many guns recently, that the appearance of one more seemed nothing of consequence. She stood and watched calmly as he pulled the trigger.

The gunshot was deafening. He had aimed straight at Grave's crotch. Graves crumpled.

Eric yelled. "Payback!"

Amy realized she had been standing completely still watching this all unfold as if in slow motion. "This is shock," a voice said in her head. "This is what shock feels like. You are in shock." She really wished the voice could stop repeating "shock"—it was starting to get annoying. Graves, still lying on the floor, pulled out his gun and shot Eric in the chest. At that point, she did stop thinking about shock, turned, and dived behind the first row of seats. Debbie was already back there.

They shared a moment of step-sisterly camaraderie as the explosions of gunfire nearly deafened them. Then, as soon as it had started, it stopped.

In retrospect, Amy should not have peeked out from behind the seats, but she did. She'd kind of expected everyone to be dead. And indeed, Eric did look dead, lying unmoving on the floor. Graves lay on the floor, a hole in the front of his trousers. Dick Storm's bicep was oozing blood and there seemed to be another bullet in his shoulder. Tommy was untouched. They were still holding their guns, but they'd frozen in place.

Debbie popped up beside her. "They're going to have to put in new carpet before *Hamilton*." Then she lost her ability to speak. Amy assumed that reaction was because of the demon standing in the middle of the men.

His face was still beautiful, but now green and scaled, with little spikes coming out of it. He had unfurled his wings—they were featherless and similarly green and leathery. In his hand, he held a glowing, red sword. His voice boomed through the empty performance hall. "I am the fallen angel, Lucael. You will all die by my hand, and I will take you to Hell as my trophies."

The demon stopped for a moment and surveyed the room. For a brief second, his eyes fell on Amy. "You have all been betrayed by the forces of good, specifically by this woman." With a twitch of his finger, Amy was pulled into the air, out from behind the row of seats, by an invisible force. Debbie tried to grab her leg and hold her down, but with a gesture of his other hand, the demon knocked her away.

Still suspended in midair, Amy yelled, "I knew you were evil with a name like Lucael,"

The demon stopped, looking exasperated. "Look, it's like I said before, there aren't really good and evil names. Just because my name sounds kind of like Lucifer isn't why I went bad. In fact, his actual name is Samael, Lucifer's just a nickname. So can we just drop it, please?"

"Whatever," Amy said. Convinced Lucael was about to take his long-ass talons and literally rip her a new one. This was no time to argue semantics.

"This woman," Lucael continued, "is a holy warrior. She insinuated her way into your group. She wormed her way into your confidences."

Somehow, David was still conscious. He looked up at Amy. "Really, Amy? You? I trusted you. I bared my fucking soul to you. We could have helped each other."

Amy bit her lip. "Look, David. I'm sorry. I didn't know who to trust. If we'd met under different circumstances..." She let her statement trail off. She wasn't really sure what else to say. She'd gone from fearing David to trusting him in such a short time. He'd turned out not to be a monster.

"Fuck you!" David yelled. He aimed his gun, and as Amy waited for the bullets to strike her body, they slammed into Lucael instead.

"Ow!" The demon turned and gave David a nasty look. "Really? I'm a fucking demon."

Graves grinned at him. "Still hurts, though, doesn't it?"

Tommy shot Lucael a couple times as well.

Lucael turned and gave Tommy a nasty look. "What was that for?"

Tommy looked rather pleased with himself. "I just got tired of pulling guns all the time and not getting to shoot anyone."

The demon raised his sword, presumably to cut David in half, but a spotlight hit him from up above. The demon looked up at the light and blinked. Then the beam refocused to the stage.

14

The Exorcists

A singsong voice echoed through the Civic Center. *"Regna terrae, cantate Deo, psallite Cernunnos."* The curtain blocking the stage dropped to the floor revealing a group of Catholic priests behind an altar loaded down with crosses and bibles. They had the little white collars and everything. The three in the front leaned over their bibles, chanting in Latin. Behind them stood another row. These priests were holding shotguns and rifles.

The demon Lucael must have lost his concentration, because Amy dropped to the floor. She managed to land on her feet, but she landed off balance and sat down hard in the first row of seats.

Storm looked on in disbelief. *"Capax Dei?* I didn't think they were real."

Lucael strode up to the stage. "They're not real. Just a story they tell to scare little Satanists. You all better run, priests. I'm getting mad."

One of the priests on the stage threw a bowl of water at the approaching demon.

"Now I'm wet," Lucael said. "I'm mad, and I'm wet."

Apparently, the holy water thing didn't work. Either that or the priest was just throwing regular water.

Maybe the water was a signal, because the other priests chose this moment to open up with the rifles and the shotguns. The sound was deafening. The demon struggled against their bombardment, and they managed to hold him back. He took a step back, then another. He dropped one knee to the floor.

As soon as the bullets started flying, Dick Storm grabbed Eric by his sleeve. Eric's shirt ripped open, revealing a bulletproof vest similar to the one Amy wore. Helping Eric with one hand and grabbing his large suitcase of money with the other, Storm ran up the aisle, showing impressive stamina for an older man. A stray bullet struck his hand. He screamed and dropped the suitcase. He pulled Eric closer to his body and ran faster.

Amy had dropped to the ground to avoid the gunfire, but now she noticed something odd about the priest on the right side of the stage. He had a sizable chin dimple, like she could see it from thirty feet away —it could only be Justice Labrador. The one in the center doing all the chanting was Mike, the cop who came from a family of priests. The priest to Justice's right was petite and Hispanic—Holden.

After a couple minutes of concentrated firing, the cops' guns clicked empty. Holden picked up a sword and lobbed it in her general direction. "Get him, Amy!"

The sword landed a few feet to Amy's right. She felt the tingle inside her body. She stooped down and picked it up. Coming up from the ground, she swung it in a wide arc, toward the demon.

Lucael blocked the sword of Zorro with his red, glowing blade, and the Zorro sword disintegrated into dust. He roared and fully extended his wings to their full height, making him seem about ten feet tall. "I am going to kill every last one of—"

A hammer, not like Thor's hammer, but a large framing hammer, slammed into the side of Lucael's head, wielded by David Graves. Amy remembered a story about David beating his Calltelestar predecessor to death with a hammer. Apparently, there was some truth to the story.

She took a few steps back as Graves pummeled the demon with numerous blows, until finally, the demon cried out in frustration. "Just my luck. My first day as a demon, and I'm attacked by the fucking *Capax Dei*. And seriously, fuck you, Graves. A hammer, really?" He swung the red sword, catching the hammer's claw, and the hammer flew from Graves' hands.

Lucael grabbed Graves and picked him up by the throat.

The hammer flopped across the carpet to rest by the first row of seats. Amy ran over and picked it up. It was huge in her hand, and the words, "Stanford Fatboy XXXL" were written across the side. Once again, power tingled inside her body, but this time, that power seemed to resonate with the hammer.

From behind the seats, Debbie grabbed Amy's arm. "What are you doing? You're going to get killed."

"Maybe," Amy said, "but this is why I'm here." She gripped the hammer tightly, leaned into the three steps between her and Lucael, and swung the framing hammer in an upwards arc that caught the demon in the crotch.

The demon dropped Graves and his sword to cover himself with his hands. He screamed, "Oh, sweet Christ! I mean, Satan." He growled. "This time I really am going to—"

Amy still didn't know if angels had genitals, but it was obviously a sensitive area. Since he was leaning down to cover his junk, Amy hit him in the mouth this time. It knocked him back.

"Enough talking." Amy raised the hammer to strike again. "Let's fight."

Picking his sword up, the demon straightened, spat out a fang, and brought its sword down. Amy caught the blade with the hammer. He reversed his swing and she caught it again, nearly forcing the sword back at him.

Amy swung the hammer at the demon's face, breaking off a couple of the little spikes protruding from his cheeks.

Just as Amy finished her attack, Graves reached up, grabbed the demon's trousers at the hips and pulled them to the floor. It turned out Angels really did have genitalia. With the green, scaly skin, it kind of looked like a little garden snake.

"Screw this." Lucael scrambled backward away from her, struggling to pull up his pants. "I'm out of here." He disappeared leaving just the rotting egg odor of sulfur behind.

There was a moment of silence, or at least Amy assumed it was silence, as her ears were still ringing quite badly from all the shooting. Everyone remaining looked around as if they expected another demon to tear through the floor and start attacking them, but all Amy heard was the front door closing, no doubt Dick and Eric making their escape.

○ ○ ○

Outside, Eric and Storm leaned on each other as they limped towards the car. Eric actually felt pretty good now that the pain from the shot to his vest was receding. Storm, however, had a hole in his hand where the stray bullet had struck, and he was quickly losing blood.

"What are we going to do now, my love?" Eric asked Storm. "Has this finally convinced you never to do business with those telemarketing bastards?"

Storm grabbed the handkerchief from his shirt pocket and wrapped it around his hand. "Yes, Eric. No more deals with Calltelestar. Maybe we can get Time Warner to buy us out. Now, no more talk. I do believe I need the hospital. I'm feeling a little lightheaded."

○ ○ ○

Amy plopped down in one of the theater seats.

Holden jumped down from the stage and joined her. "Are you all right?"

She nodded. "Maybe a few bumps and bruises, but yes, I'm relatively unharmed." To be polite she added, "How are you?"

"Physically, I'm fine. I'm a little messed up in the head though. The whole angel and demon thing, it's not that I didn't believe you, but it's different to see it up close, and in the same venue where I saw *My Fair Lady*."

Amy looked up on the stage, where Justice and Holden's cop friends were congratulating each other. "Then why did you bring the phony exorcism crew?"

"That was all Mike's idea. His family wanted him to be a priest, you know. He studied for it and everything. He figured the Satanists would be more scared of priest commandos than they would be of uniformed police officers. I just sort of went along with his idea. Plus, we were coming in heavily armed, so we had that going for us if the priest thing didn't impress them." He made a face. "I wasn't expecting the demon."

She reached over and pulled the white collar out of his shirt. It was cardboard.

Holden grinned. "The backing from a Little Debbie snack cake." He shrugged.

213

Amy looked again and saw he was telling the truth. In fact, there was still a little chocolate stuck to the back.

Graves limped over and nodded to the hammer. "Can I get that back?"

Amy nodded. "Yes, but how are you even walking?"

He pulled down the front of his pants and showed her something bulky and black.

"Am I supposed to know what that is?" Amy asked.

"Kevlar nut cup. Better safe than sorry."

Holden reached for the object. "I've always wanted to see one of those."

Graves stepped back and pulled his pants up. "I'd be happy to show it to you some other time."

She handed Graves the hammer and watched as he limped over to inspect one of the Calltellestar money bags. Despite the Kevlar, he was clearly hurting.

With Graves gone, Justice joined them. "Amy, are you—"

"Yes, fine. Holden and I were just through all that. How did you end up here?"

He grinned. "Holden called me to find out where the meeting was going to be."

Amy nodded. "And you knew this because..."

"I've kind of been seeing Debbie for the last week or so. You know when I said I wasn't just dating you to make her jealous? That may have been a little white lie."

Amy kind of wanted to hit him. "No, Justice. *Your ass looks good in those jeans* is a little white lie. What you're describing is an all-out deception." She took a deep breath and sighed. "But I don't care, because as I said at the beginning, we had no relationship. I didn't want to date you anyway. I hope you're very happy with Debbie."

She really doubted he would be, but she was okay with that. Despite her nice words, he was lucky she'd given Graves the hammer.

"Speaking of Debbie..." Debbie said, crawling over into the front row of seats, which was kind of impressive in a long skirt. "Shouldn't you be checking on me?"

He shrugged. "Nah, you're tough."

They were momentarily distracted by David Graves using his hammer to beat a computer backup tape into tiny pieces. Then he tore a chunk of paper and ate it. "Soul contract," he explained as he chewed. "If I burn it, they might still manage to magic it back together. I'm going to be extra careful. I'm not even going to pass this whole thing in the same toilet."

"Okay," Holden said, "putting that aside for a moment, it seems to me that there's a whole lot of Satanist money here, and not that many of us."

"That Aldi bag is mine," Tommy said. "I'm keeping it. Actually, Bitcoin dropped twenty percent after I cashed that out, so if I reinvest it now, I'm probably going to make money on the rebound."

"That seems fair," Amy said. She glanced around. "Um, what should we do with the rest of the money?"

For a long moment, everyone was quiet. Then David said, "Technically, it does belong to Calltelestar and Mediastorm, but if no one argues, I think we should just say, 'fuck them,' and split it up."

Amy did a little math in her head. "If everyone got a share, there should still be eighteen million dollars in cash, and just ten of us left, assuming Tommy's happy with just taking back his two million."

Tommy nodded amicably. "Sure, I'm good."

"So," Amy said, "we have the place for the rest of the afternoon. We might as well divide up the rest of the money."

"Great idea, Sis," Debbie said, "but if you don't mind, could you take care of Justice's and my share? You see, I already have this plane chartered to take me to Japan and a very nice hotel booked on Calltelestar's credit card—"

Amy sighed. "Yes, go."

Just as long as she didn't go near the idea of Debbie and Justice doing it.

"I doubt we'll even leave the room," Justice added.

"Ew," Amy said. "Yes. Please go."

Debbie smiled. "And when we get back, we'll help you all set up some numbered accounts in the Caymans."

As they were leaving, Holden turned to David. "I don't think we've been introduced. I'm Amy's friend, Holden. You work for the Calltelestar Satanists, don't you?"

David shrugged. "Up until about five minutes ago, yes." As if to punctuate this, he tore another chunk off his contract and started chewing it.

Holden continued. "Do you think they're going to come after us?"

David thought about this for a moment. "I can see what you mean. Mediastorm can swallow a loss of a few million easy, but Calltelestar is going to be more upset about their money. I've seen them kill people for a lot less. However, when I slipped my soul contract..." He held up what was left of the document in question. "I didn't just steal my own. I went ahead and took all of them. At the moment, I literally have possession of most of their souls." He pointed to the little chunks of plastic and spaghetti of magnetic tape on the floor. "And those are the backups. I think I can keep them off our backs." He stuffed another piece of paper into his mouth. He had a lot of chewing to do. To Amy, it looked like the document was a dozen pages at least, and he had only finished the first one.

15

Unemployed

The next day, Amy went to work to find the receptionist gone. As she walked down the back hallway to her
office, she saw Tommy's door open, and she peeked in.
"Hey, Tommy. How are you doing?"

Tommy was feeding three cheap paper shredders
lined up on his desk. "Oh, hi, Amy! I was just packing
up my things. I'm going to head back to Bolivia. I've
overstayed my welcome in this country." He slipped a
stack of papers into a shredder.

"What happened?"

"Well..." He stuffed his laptop into a briefcase and
closed it. "I ordered a Bolivian hit squad at the last
minute, because I was going to rob everyone yesterday, and they kind of got caught at the border with
nothing on them but a stack of US currency and my

address." He walked over to a wall safe she hadn't known was there and took out a stack of money. "Here's fifty thousand dollars. Consider it your severance pay and whatever I owe you for the week. I threw in those *Hamilton* tickets we talked about."

"Sure." The Midwesterner in her wanted to resist taking so much money for so little time, especially with the stack of money she'd taken home after the shootout. However, she'd had to put up with a lot of crap from Tommy, including seeing his wang, so she felt entitled.

He tapped a thick manila envelope on his desk. "These are the keys to the building. I paid for a year's lease. You can use the office for the rest of the lease if you want, but when you're done, just make sure the doors are locked and throw the keys on the reception desk. Oh, and take anything you want, furniture, computers, whatever. I'm abandoning it."

She nodded to the open closet door in the corner of his office. "What about all those machine guns?"

"They aren't machine guns. They're semi-automatic rifles, AR15s. They were for the thugs that got stuck at the border. Keep them, sell them, whatever you want."

"I'm sure I know someone who wants them." Her dad and a couple of his friends belonged to a shooting club. He'd know what to do with them.

She walked into her office and looked through her things. She really hadn't had time to add anything personal, so she loaded her computer onto her office chair and rolled it down to her car. She kept the keys though. She might want to come back for a desk. One of Holden's buddies probably had a truck. Sure, she was a millionaire now, but that was no reason to turn down free stuff.

Once she was in the car, she called her father.

"Hi Dad. This is America. I have some news."

"What's that, darlin?"

"I'm unemployed again."

"Well, that's nothing to worry about, is it? That's the way you kids do things with the whole gig economy thing. Of course, your stepmother, well, she doesn't see things that way. Don't worry your head, though. I'll keep paying your bills and give you some time to find a job."

"Oh, no. Actually, I want to take over my credit card payments and rent. I made a bit of money at this last job, and I think I'll be all right without help."

"That must have been a good deal Debbie got you into. She just called me this morning from Kyoto, Japan. She's shacked up with some lawyer over there. She says that when they come back, they're going to get married and buy me out. I'm going to be retiring. Can you believe that?"

"Well, that's great." Amy actually had never thought of her father retiring. She'd imagined he'd work until he died.

"Actually, I'm going to keep a hand in..."

Amy nodded to herself. Of course, he was.

"Some of these older fellas, they don't like change. I'll still do the handshaking and social calls. But there's a lot of younger fellas around here buying out or inheriting their daddies' farms, and they probably won't mind a lady lawyer, especially if she's a local. Her city boy's probably going to be stuck indoors doing a lot of paperwork, though."

"I hope that works out for them." Amy said, and to her surprise, she actually meant it. "Hey, are you or any of your buddies interested in some free AR15s?"

"How many?"

"Three."

"Why is someone giving them away? Were they used to commit a crime? I am an officer of the court, you know."

"They were probably *going* to be used to commit a crime but weren't. The owner had to leave the country fast."

"Sure, I'll take them."

"Okay, I'll bring them with me next time I visit." After a moment of silence, she said, "Well, that's all the news I have."

"Me too, darlin. I guess I'll talk to you later."

"Love you, Dad. And tell Patty... hi."

"I'll do that. Bye now."

○ ○ ○

That night, Amy fell asleep watching a documentary about Tommy Norman on her new computer and sipping rum and Diet Coke. In a half-awake state, she felt like she was being watched and opened her eyes to find Ottoel standing in front of her.

"Where the fuck have you been?"

He smiled. "Technically, I'm not here now. You're dreaming. And to answer your question, I'm kind of dead."

"Kind of?"

"Yeah, Lucael killed me so I couldn't help you at the Civic Center. I'm really sorry about that. I never saw it coming."

"And now you're 'kind of' dead?"

He nodded. "Yeah. He killed the body that was housing my spirit. I've ordered a new one, but there's quite a backlog. It may take a few decades since I don't have an urgent need. We have a saying up there. Satan might have invented bureaucracy, but we're working hard to perfect it." He looked around her apartment and shook his head. "Since this is a dream, and we can be anywhere we want." He snapped his fingers, and they were in a Mexican restaurant.

Amy rolled her eyes. "Oh, come on, are you still going to say you've never seen *Karma*?"

"What do you mean?" He loaded up a tortilla chip with salsa and stuffed it in his mouth. "I just like the chips."

"The first time we see Metatron in the film, he snaps his fingers and teleports them to a Mexican restaurant."

"Metatron, like the Transformer?"

She raised an eyebrow. "Was that a joke?"

"Yes. Apparently, I need to work on my delivery. That joke kills upstairs. It's a little obvious, but any joke that's not a thousand years old is a novelty. Although I hear you shouldn't say it anywhere around Metatron. Seriously though, the restaurant is just a co-incidence. I love chips and salsa."

"Bummer about getting killed. Well, at least you tried. I'm really sorry the merger didn't go through."

"Oh, yeah, the merger. That's nice. But more importantly, we got David out of his contract." He stuffed another chip into his mouth.

"David?"

"David Graves, yes. This was all about him. You see, he freed another Calltelestar employee from his contract a few years ago, sacrificing himself in the process. This whole operation was about positioning David to get into the Calltelestar vault to take back the contract for his soul. I assume he did, didn't he? I'm a little out of the loop, with no body and my immediate superior becoming a demon."

"I saw him eat it myself."

"That's for the best. They are really good at recovering documents."

"You could have told me that I was there to save Graves."

He nodded. "Maybe I was supposed to. I just followed Lucael's orders. He could have been lying the whole time. Since he's defected, I guess we'll never know. I could ask his superiors, but I'm not exactly in favor right now." He rolled his eyes. "Like it's my fault my boss turned evil."

Amy tried the salsa. It was hot, but they were in a dream, so she tried to will a blended margarita into existence.

221

A waitress stopped and set one down in front of her. "Need anything else, sweetie?"

She shook her head. "That's perfect." She turned to Ottoel. "I still can't believe this whole thing was for the betterment of David Graves?"

"What did you think this was all about? You? We needed you for a task, so we called on you." He smiled. "And you did exactly what we hoped you'd do. You pulled David out of the Satanist shell he'd built around his life and freed him from the contractual bindings holding him back." He held up a menu. "Would you like to order?"

"What's the point? I'm dreaming. It's not like it would provide nourishment."

"Zero calories," he pointed out hopefully. "Besides I don't have a body anymore, so this is probably my last meal for a while. I can't lurk around in people's dreams hoping for a free meal."

"I guess you're welcome in my dreams. Especially if there's going to be guilt-free dessert."

He shook his head. "Actually, the fried ice cream here is terrible."

Amy thought about arguing. It was her dream. Couldn't she make the fried ice cream better? She sighed. "Okay, then." She waved at the waitress. "Another margarita."

○ ○ ○

After one week without a job, Amy was bored. Sure, she'd been unemployed before, but there'd always been the desperation her father might cut off her credit cards and the knowledge she'd have to get another job soon. Now, she didn't have to, and she had nothing to do but drink and watch YouTube videos about the Mandela Effect, which she now knew was mainly just Tommy. It was driving her crazy.

She spent a lot of time with Holden on his days off —he and the other police officers had made an agreement that none of them would quit the force right away. If some of them wanted to quit, they would stagger their resignations, to quell any suspicions they'd come into money.

Amy briefly considered going back to school to get her paralegal degree. She even toyed with the idea of being Debbie's and Justice's assistant. She really didn't mind the idea of going back to Holstein now that she wouldn't have to live at home or marry a rich farmer to survive.

One night, when Holden was pulling back-to-back shifts, she got bored and decided to go to Rosa. As she was drinking rum and Diet Coke and snacking on fried calamari, David Graves walked up to her table. He still had a bit of a limp.

"Mind if I join you?" He slowly lowered himself into a chair without waiting for her reply. "My nuts are killing me. At least they've returned to their usual size. The day after the gunfight, the were swollen up like a grapefruit."

"So," she said, "they let you keep the restaurant?"

He shrugged. "It's legally in my name." He took a piece of her calamari and popped it in his mouth.

"And how are things with your fiancée?"

"Oddly, better than ever. It turns out she was pissed off at me because I was trying to be a good Satanist and make her father happy. Those two have a rough history, you know?" He lowered his voice. "Confidentially, I'd been sleeping on the couch a lot, but now things are back on track in the bedroom department. I just have to remember to take my pain pills." He then added, "For my balls."

"Good for you," she said quickly, afraid he might elaborate further. For some reason, perhaps the release of his contract, she didn't find him that attractive anymore, which somehow made him more likable. "And what about your future father-in-law?"

"As in, will he send people to kill you to get back his money?" He smiled. "I don't think we have anything

223

to worry about on that account. Sure, he's pissed, but I technically own the souls of everyone in his organization, so he has to be nice to me."

Amy nodded. "That's one fucked-up family dynamic you've got there, Graves."

David shrugged. "Everyone rebels against their parents a little. When you're half-demon, I think rebellion comes a little easier." He paused and munched another piece of calamari. "So, changing the subject, I wanted to ask you a question. You were Tommy's office manager, correct?"

She shrugged. "Technically, I suppose. That's what he called me."

"Would you be interested in doing that sort of work again?"

"Do you mean working with a bunch of Satanists or running an office? I could maybe do some office work."

He absentmindedly took another piece of calamari and popped it in his mouth. Then as if realizing what he'd done, he waved over a waitress. "Carol, could you get us some more calamari, and please comp Miss Am... Amy's bill." When he was done with the waitress, he turned back to Amy. "I'm thinking of starting a charity."

"A charity? What for?"

"I've spent the last few years being a bad person and doing bad things. It made me miserable. Now, I'd like to give something back. I like the idea of using a bunch of Satanists' money to do some good in the world. I'm not one hundred percent sure what kind of charity I'd like to start, but I have the money to start one, so I guess I just need some office space and a cause."

"I can help with the office space, but don't you have to be passionate about a cause to become involved with it?"

"What about inner-city kids? I hear they have a hard life." He paused. "Global warming? I hear clean drinking water is a big deal."

"Maybe we should put a pin in that. I'm sure it will come to you in time."

"All right. But what do you think about working for me?"

She nodded. "That sounds nice. Sign me up."

About the Author

Shannon Ryan lives in Marion, Iowa. He writes weird, funny stories in the urban fantasy genre, featuring satanic telemarketers and awkward vampires.

In addition to writing, he enjoys making furniture and other items out of wood, writing computer programs, designing models for 3d printing, editing books for others, and playing with kitties.

Minion of Evil

Have you ever wondered if your boss is evil?

David Graves is having a bad life. A bill collector is threatening him with grievous bodily harm. His girlfriend thinks he's an incompetent loser. His human resources manager, a creature of nightmare, is sexually harassing him. And when he finally meets a girl he likes, she seems more interested in rebuilding engines and committing random acts of violence.

Still, David thinks he is doing all right—until he discovers his bosses are Satanists and his employment contract dooms him to an eternity of telemarketing and damnation...

Minion of Evil is frightfully accurate portrayal of identity theft, computer hacking, wrench wenches, monomaniacal supervisors, and what really goes on behind closed doors in customer service.

https://weirdauthor.com/evil

MINION OF EVIL

SHANNON RYAN

Shannon Ryan

Fangs for Nothing

Not everyone who gets turned into a vampire becomes a sexy rock star.

At twenty-seven, Vincent Lester still looks seventeen, acne and all. He lives in his parents' basement, playing PlayStation and barely surviving by licking the blood off raw hamburger trays. His parents nag him to find a day job, but he's afraid the sun will make him burst into flame.

One night at the bar, Vinny picks up a drunk girl, literally, and gets his first taste of fresh, human blood. Then things get really weird.

http://weirdauthor.com/fangs

Panic No More

Even the best families can have dark secrets.

Some people would say Nick Baker has it all: the trust fund, the family connections, and the country club membership. However, the Baker dynasty is in decline, and being a Baker comes with obligations as well as a family history of insanity.

Already prone to panic attacks, when Nick sees a supernatural creature dancing outside his office window, he wonders if he's just hallucinating or suffering a complete mental collapse. However, the creature is all too real, and it has come to collect on a promise made by one of Nick's ancestors, the secret of the Baker's success. Nick must choose between thwarting the ambitions of his family or facing the wrath of an ancient god.

https://weirdauthor.com/panic